To Jeri,

This was a lot of fun to write and to research. I hope you enjoy it.

A Portrait of Murder

A Portrait of Murder

D.E. Gilmore

Copyright © 2011 by D.E. Gilmore.

Library of Congress Control Number:		2011906094
ISBN:	Hardcover	978-1-4628-5935-1
	Softcover	978-1-4628-5934-4
	Ebook	978-1-4628-5936-8

All rights reserved. No part of this book may be reproduced or transmitted in any form or by any means, electronic or mechanical, including photocopying, recording, or by any information storage and retrieval system, without permission in writing from the copyright owner.

This is a work of fiction. Names, characters, places and incidents either are the product of the author's imagination or are used fictitiously, and any resemblance to any actual persons, living or dead, events, or locales is entirely coincidental.

This book was printed in the United States of America.

To order additional copies of this book, contact:
Xlibris Corporation
1-888-795-4274
www.Xlibris.com
Orders@Xlibris.com
97232

Contents

Chapter 1	Elko, Nevada (1872)	7
Chapter 2	Springfield, Illinois (Present Day)	10
Chapter 3	The Sunday Supplement	13
Chapter 4	The California Trail (1850)	19
Chapter 5	Springfield, Illinois	26
Chapter 6	The California Trail (1850)	31
Chapter 7	Elko, Nevada (Present Day)	40
Chapter 8	Humboldt River Valley (1850)	45
Chapter 9	Elko, Nevada (Present Day)	51
Chapter 10	Humboldt Wells, Utah Territory (1850)	57
Chapter 11	Elko, Nevada (Present Day)	62
Chapter 12	California Trail (1850)	70
Chapter 13	The Bed-and-Breakfast on Silver Street	76
Chapter 14	The Wall Defile (1850)	82
Chapter 15	Marshall Dillon	89
Chapter 16	Carson Pass (1850)	97
Chapter 17	Elko (Present Day)	104
Chapter 18	San Francisco (1859)	112
Chapter 19	Elko (Present Day)	119
Chapter 20	Virginia City (1860)	126
Chapter 21	Silver Street (Present Day)	134
Chapter 22	Virginia City (1866)	142
Chapter 23	Virginia City (Present Day)	150
Chapter 24	Virginia City (January 1872)	156
Chapter 25	Stockmen's Hotel (Present Day)	162
Chapter 26	Virginia City (1872)	168
Chapter 27	Boston (Present Day)	174
Chapter 28	Wadsworth, Nevada (1872)	180
Chapter 29	Elko, Nevada (Present Day)	184

Chapter 30	Humboldt River (1872)	190
Chapter 31	Elko, Nevada (Present Day)	193
Chapter 32	Winnemucca, Nevada (1872)	200
Chapter 33	Elko (Present Day)	204
Chapter 34	Elko, Nevada (1872)	209
Chapter 35	Elko (Present Day)	211
Chapter 36	Virginia City (1875)	217

CHAPTER 1

Elko, Nevada (1872)

Eli Wilkes sat on the settee in the salon of the house on Silver Street. It was a comfortable chair, upholstered in brown velvet with thickly padded oak armrests, well suited for the clientele of the bordello. He was turned to his side, looking at a painting on the wall behind him. It was a small framed picture, and in the center of the painting was a portrait of Eli. In the painting, he stood in front of the settee on which he was now sitting. He had a small, knowing smile on his face and was wearing a new suit with a sculptured vest. His right hand intruded into the vest. He was standing straight-backed, formally, and the blue striped suit complimented his recently barbered blond hair.

Eli Wilkes was wearing that same suit as he sat on the settee, contemplating his visage in the picture. He seemed satisfied with what he saw. In the portrait, there were two pictures on the wall behind him above the settee, set off against the green-and-pink floral wallpaper of the room. The two pictures—each of a different woman—were small, round, and delicate in their tiny frames. The entire portrait displayed a dark warmth that was equally captured in the room that he sat.

This is a good place to die, Eli thought to himself as he glanced around the room. It is a room that has inspired men to carnal depths, has diminished their woes, has delayed their fears, has warmed their hearts, and has temporarily quelled their longings for other places. It is a good place to leave a remembrance of oneself.

It was then that he heard the commotion outside the room, the scurrying of covered feet and the small female cries of fear. The door opened. Eli saw the outline of something protruding into the room. A hand holding something! A gun!

Then the door swung wide open, and a figure cautiously stepped into the room, surveying the room as he entered. The man was of medium height, dressed in range clothes. His hat was broad and weatherworn, and he wore a maroon cotton shirt covered by a brown leather vest. A green sweat-soaked and dusty kerchief was slung around his neck and tied carelessly, and he wore dark corduroy pants above muddied medium-heeled boots. He wore no spurs, which struck Eli as odd as the outlines of the spurs were clearly visible in the caked-on mud of the boots. Then Eli realized that the man had removed his spurs to walk more silently. When had the man done that? Eli wondered.

The eyes of the man in the hat settled on Eli, and for a moment, he appeared to contemplate what to do. Decided, he stepped further into the room, allowing another man to enter behind him. This man was older, taller, and thicker but dressed in much the same manner, except that he wore an overcoat and carried a rifle. It was clear that they had ridden hard to get here, as the dirt and grime of the trail still clung to their clothing. The men stared hard at Eli who rose to his feet.

The two riders seemed to have an unspoken understanding as the older man leaned his rifle against the doorjamb and drew a long-barreled revolver from under his coat. He aimed the revolver at Eli, his eyes cold, gray, and emotionless. He fired one round, which hit Eli in the chest between the cravat tie at his collar and the upward sweep of the sculptured vest. Eli looked startled for a moment, looked down at the red stain creeping onto his white ruffled shirt, and collapsed onto the multicolored oriental carpet. In a second's time, his eyes clouded over and became sightless as blood pooled on the carpet beneath him.

The younger man strolled over to Eli, bent down, and rummaged through Eli's pockets. He found a gold watch in the vest pocket, stared at it for a moment, stood up, and turned to the older man. He tossed the watch to the older man, who also glanced at it and placed it into his coat pocket. The older man holstered his pistol, picked up the rifle, and the two men strode out of the room and out of the house. As they rode away, a scream could be heard inside the house on Silver Street.

CHAPTER 2

Springfield, Illinois (Present Day)

Elizabeth Ryder glanced at her brother to see his expression. She had been crying and was holding the handkerchief near her eyes to disguise her looking at him peripherally. Jason Ryder, at twenty one, was two years older than Elizabeth; he stood stoically, staring at the ground at the grave in front of them. Elizabeth could not tell by his expression what he was feeling or thinking. He seemed like a statue—calm, cold, and implacable. How like their father, she thought, watching him. He even looked like their father or, rather, like the pictures of their father when he was younger.

Roland Ryder should not be dead now! He was only forty-five and had been perfectly healthy until six months ago. Then came the cancer. It was a horrible disease that had robbed Roland of his vitality; of his wit, humor, and spontaneity; and finally, his life. Elizabeth remembered her father before the cancer. She remembered the very day that he told them about his ailment and his expression of pained fear, not for himself but of how she and Jason would react. He called them into the TV room of the house on Market Street, their grandmother's house, and told them about the illness. He spoke hesitantly, unsure of the words, and watched their expressions as if to gauge what to say next.

Elizabeth had cried—sobbed, actually—with huge bent-over gasps of disbelieving breaths, clutching her abdomen and sides. Her father had stepped up to her and tried to hold her, awkwardly, sincerely. Jason had stood much like he was standing now—looking down, not speaking, not reacting in any discernable way. It made Elizabeth angry now, as it had done then.

Their grandmother had taken to her bed upstairs. Their father had told her before he had told them, before they had arrived to share that Sunday dinner. Elizabeth glanced now at her grandmother who sat in a chair next to Jason, dressed in a plain black dress and black brimmed hat, looking so small and so old. Her grandmother's hands covered her wrinkled face, which was bowed down almost to her chest. She was quietly crying, her small body quivering every few seconds with the ejaculations of emotional pain.

Elizabeth thought then about her grandmother, really for the first time since her father's dreadful disclosure those six months ago. How does one grieve one's son? How would one go on living every day thereafter, feeling the loss of one so completely intertwined into one's life? How does one live when a part of one's body, one's heart, has been ripped away and thrust into the cold earth so finally? What would her grandmother do?

These thoughts brought Elizabeth back to herself. Indeed, what would she do? Her father had been incredibly intertwined in her life as well. Since their mother had abandoned them when Elizabeth was two years old, it had only been her father, her grandmother, and her brother. They had been her whole world really. Jason had left to go into the army at eighteen but had finished his service and had returned two months before their father's illness. It was supposed to be like before Jason's departure—a solid family.

"Come on, Liz." Her brother was tugging on her sleeve. "Let's go. We need to get Grandma home."

Elizabeth realized that the graveside service had concluded. Her grandmother had stood weakly, shaking as if on weary legs, and was trying to step around the folding chair. Jason was trying to guide her with a solid grasp on her arm, patiently waiting for her to collect herself enough to walk. The few people who had attended the funeral were already leaving the cemetery.

Back at their grandmother's house, Elizabeth and Jason gratefully and gracefully accepted the plates of food offered by those few neighbors and friends of their father and grandmother. Their grandmother sat in the corner of the TV room in her swivel rocking chair and rocked slowly, silently, without looking up. She would tearfully mutter something softly, almost inaudibly, when someone grabbed her small hand to express his or her sympathy. They would quickly back away, not knowing what else to say or do. People milled around for a while, waiting for the appropriate time to leave. After a while, it was just Elizabeth, Jason, and their grandmother in the room. They sat in chairs in close proximity to each other but did not speak. It was as if this was where the real mourning was to begin.

CHAPTER 3

The Sunday Supplement

Jason slammed the door a little too loudly to leave it without comment.

"What's your problem?" Elizabeth asked, peering over the top of the newspaper's Sunday Supplement.

"Nothing," he stated as he put down the baseball glove and bat. He had been to the park with his friends to play a scratch game of baseball; now he slunk sullenly into the chair by the fireplace. "Where's Grandma?"

"She's upstairs taking a nap."

Jason and Elizabeth had moved into their grandmother's house soon after their father's funeral. Both had realized that their grandmother needed their attention and companionship now more than ever, and each was concerned that she had become so old almost overnight. Prior to their father's illness and ultimate demise, their grandmother had seemed so vital. She had volunteered at the local nursing home, bringing her piano and singing skills to the shut-ins and coordinating bingo games three days a week. All of that ended with Roland's death.

Roland Ryder was Agnes Ryder's only child. After her husband's death, Agnes inserted herself into her son's life with a ferocity that comes with desperate need. Roland accepted his mother's interference in his life because he realized that his children needed a woman's care, and he was unwilling to compromise their happiness in the hands of a stranger. His work with the phone company kept him busy during the weekdays and on some weekends, leaving his children unattended for a time after school. Having his mother live with them met many needs, the least of which was a constant, stable, and forceful presence in the home.

The children and Roland benefited from Agnes's attendance in their lives. She cooked, cleaned, polished, washed clothes, and mothered everyone as only one's own mother/grandmother could do. Shortly thereafter, the family realized that Roland's house was too small for all of them, and they made the move back to Agnes's home. It was bigger by two bedrooms, one of which was in the basement and was better organized to suit Agnes. Roland's little house, which was only three blocks away, then became a rental until Jason finished his military service. He and Elizabeth, upon his return, moved to that house to have some adult-child privacy away from the prying eyes of their father and grandmother.

Even so, they came every Sunday to their grandmother's home for Sunday dinner. It was a tradition that none were willing to forego, especially as it was the one guaranteed home-cooked meal of the week for both Jason and Elizabeth. Additionally, it was a time of family contentedness where each could sit in the den, read the Sunday paper, and speak only if desired. It felt good to each of them and cemented the solidness of family.

"Bad game?" Elizabeth asked without much sincere interest.

"No. It was fine," Jason responded through his steepled fingers, his thumbs pressed against his forehead. He was slouched in the chair as if all energy had been drained from his body. "They were just giving me a hard time about losing my job."

Jason had worked for almost a year on a construction site in East Springfield as a carpenter's assistant. It was a good job that didn't pay well but allowed him to learn a trade. The construction industry in Illinois was hit as hard as elsewhere by the recent downturn of the economy, and Jason had been subsequently laid off. He was thinking about using his GI Bill to go to college but hadn't shared that information with anyone outside of the family.

Elizabeth, at nineteen, had taken a year off after high school to work in a dental office in order to earn money for college. She was scheduled to begin her freshman year of college in September at the University of Illinois in Champaigne. She had quit her job two weeks ago to enjoy the summer and to get ready for school.

"Did you read this article in the Sunday Supplement?" she queried.

"Nope," came the languid reply.

Elizabeth continued, undaunted.

"It's about James Vanderlin and his stepson Eli Wilkes."

"Uh-huh." The response was automatic and uninterested.

"You remember James Vanderlin!" Elizabeth would not be deterred. "He is an ancestor of ours. Dad used to talk about him. He made millions of dollars in that Comstock gold find in Nevada back in the 1800s."

"Yah, I remember. So what?"

"Well, this article is talking about him and how he had his stepson murdered."

"Oh yah? Why did he do that?" Jason seemed slightly more interested now. He had always loved history, although not particularly his own.

"Apparently, this Eli Wilkes had stolen something from our ancestor, some kind of treasure. Wilkes's mother had married James Vanderlin, and after she died, Wilkes stole the treasure and ran off. Vanderlin sent killers after Wilkes. They caught him in Elko, Nevada, killed him, and brought back some of the treasure to Vanderlin. The article says that most of the treasure was never recovered."

"So what happened to it?"

"I don't know. It doesn't say. It says that Wilkes was killed in a bordello in Elko, and the legend is that the treasure is still hidden somewhere in that place."

Jason sat up attentively. "Do you mean the building is still there?"

"Apparently, although now it is a bed-and-breakfast place. It says that there is a painting of Wilkes on the wall, and some people speculate that it is a clue to where the treasure is hidden. It says here that Wilkes had the painting done himself before he was killed, and it still hangs on the same wall and in the same room where he was killed."

"Yah, right," Jason exclaimed doubtfully.

"I'm serious!" Elizabeth objected forcefully. "According to this article, the owner of the house has had the house renovated and restored to its original condition and décor, and uses that as an incentive for people to stay at his bed-and-breakfast. People actually stay there to try to find the treasure. It says that James Vanderlin was incredibly wealthy and that even a small part of his fortune would be worth a lot today if it was found. Back then apparently, it was not uncommon for rich people to keep their money in gold, so they think that is what is hidden in the house."

Again, Jason was incredulous. "You said the owner of the house had the place renovated. I'm sure he looked for the gold when he was working on the place. Who wouldn't?"

Elizabeth was thoughtful about Jason's suspicions. "Yes, but what is to say that the gold has to be in the house? The article simply says that the painting may be a clue to the location of the treasure. That doesn't mean that the treasure has to be in the house. It may be somewhere else nearby. Or, it could still be in the house, but in a place that no one would think to look. Someplace that wouldn't have been torn apart in the renovation."

"Like a fireplace or in a basement foundation?"

"Sure. Why not?"

"It is possible, I guess." Jason admitted.

Elizabeth and Jason were silent for a few moments while Elizabeth finished reading the article. She read silently to herself and, upon completion, folded the magazine and laid it on her lap. She stared pensively out of the window at the branches of the tree gently swaying in the breeze. The rustling leaves whispered loudly enough to be heard through the partially closed window.

Breaking the lazy silence, Elizabeth turned to Jason.

"Why don't we go there? Why don't we look for the treasure?"

Jason laughed.

"I'm serious, Jason. It would be good for us. We both love history. This concerns an ancestor of ours, so we could learn something about our family and have a great kind of vacation on top of it. We are not doing anything until the fall anyway, that is if you are going to go to school as well, and it would be fun."

Elizabeth was getting into the spirit of the adventure while Jason looked even more dubious. "It's just you and Grandma and I now. Dad told us about some of our other relatives that were related to this James Vanderlin. We could write to them or advertise on the Internet, and we could all meet in Elko at the end of the summer and have an adventure! It would be fun, and maybe we could find relatives that we would want to keep in our lives! What have we got to lose?"

"What about Grandma?" Jason asked, ever practical.

"She can come with, if she wants. Or we can ask the neighbors to look in on her, or one of her friends. We won't be gone that long, maybe a week! It would be so much fun!"

Jason considered it for several moments, doubts nimbly and obviously crossing his mind and registering in his somber eyes.

"Come on, Jason! When will we be able to do this again? Once we start school we won't have time for years, and then who knows what will happen? Once we graduate, we will start to work and have families, and then what? I don't want to look back and wish that I had done something like this. I would be mad as hell to someday read that someone had found the treasure and that I had never even tried. At least if we try, then we would be glad if someone else finds it! What do you say?" she pleaded.

Jason relented. There really was no reason to not do this. They had some money left to them after their father's death, and they really did have nothing going on until the fall. It might be fun, and god knows he would like to get away from Springfield, even if for a short while.

"All right, Sis," he capitulated. "But you are doing the writing to people and the advertising! I'm just going along to keep you out of trouble! And if these relatives of ours are a bunch of crazies, I'm leaving! Agreed?"

"Absolutely!" Elizabeth was grinning as she clapped her hands together in glee.

Jason shook his head in resignation, knowing that Elizabeth usually got her way when she really wanted something. "I will do some research on the Internet and see what I can find out about this ancestor of ours."

CHAPTER 4

The California Trail (1850)

       James Vanderlin placed the edge of his hand over his eyes to block the sun. He was peering at a rider coming over the ridge to the west, riding out of the sun toward the wagon train. The rider was carrying something large across the horn of his saddle. James turned on the back of the ox he was riding. He sat atop the ox next to the bigger ox on his right, for this was the one that needed motivating. Together, the two oxen pulled the prairie schooner-type wagon at a slow but steady pace.

  "Rider coming in," he called to Josephine, his wife of sixteen years, who rode just inside the wagon. He could hear Josie talking to their daughter Jessie who, at fifteen and a half, was fully a woman now.

  James Vanderlin had met his wife when she was seventeen and he was twenty three. He had seen her across the room at a town dance in Peoria, Illinois, and had been instantly drawn to her. Her rich flaxen hair hung to the bottom of her shapely back, just above the sway of her hips at the top of the bustle on her satin dress. The dress was deeply blue and shimmered in the soft glow of the lamps surrounding the crowded hall. Her hair caught the light and flickered like the stars against the dusk-blue sky of a summer night.

He knew then that he had to have her. But how? She was the daughter of a local magistrate, and he was a no-good rounder who had numerous clashes with the local constables. He had actually stood in front of her father to receive his fair judgment on one occasion!

It wasn't that James Vanderlin was a disadvantaged youth who was following a course not of his choosing. He was the son of a minister who pastored a small congregational church down the street from the jail. The pastor's wife had died years earlier when James was seven, leaving the pastor to raise his son and a younger daughter in the stern and unforgiving manner in which he had been raised. Reverend Vanderlin believed that his children must reflect his Christian values and reinforced this belief by frequently beating his children, especially his son. He lived in the fear that his son would bring shame on him and fail Christ by behaving badly.

Which is exactly what James did.

James Vanderlin began gambling shortly after his mother's death. He started with other boys from the neighborhood and the small one-room school. He found he had a knack with different games involving chance and, more often than not, took the other boys' money. This was not much since the boys in the neighborhood earned very little cash when they were leant out by their fathers for various labor jobs. Their fathers kept the rest of the money that the boys were not able to secret away.

With the money that he won at gambling, which usually consisted of tossing coins against a wall, James was able to buy tobacco from the back of one of the saloons nearby. He liked the idea of smoking tobacco, standing under the huge oak tree behind the church, feeling sophisticated and urbane. It gave him grandiose ideas about what he could achieve and become. He saw himself in a big city with many wealthy and respectable people fawning over him while the local toughs would come to pay tribute. It was a fanciful picture that caused him to become involved in many nefarious activities and fights through the ensuing years.

Until he saw Josephine Webberly across that crowded hall. In that first moment, he did not know that she was Judge Webberly's daughter, or he would have been too intimidated to speak to her. However, his ignorance was his triumph, for when he sidled up to her, she did not shrink away. In fact, she glanced at him challengingly and literally pushed him to the side playfully. It gave him a reason to speak to her, and he did so teasingly, flirtatiously. His coarseness was obvious, although he was intelligent and was suitably schooled. It was not his clothes—which were approved by his father although bought with means of his illegitimate labors and were not threadbare—which identified his being accustomed with street life. It was his attitude—which showed a certain disdain for the niceties of polite society, although unintentional—and his choice of a raucous vocabulary that gave him away as a ruffian.

Josephine didn't seem to mind this; as a point of fact, she actually was thrilled by it. She was bored with the fawning of the boys in her circle and considered their structured politeness unattractive. James Vanderlin was the opposite. His pretense at politeness was too forced to be ultimately believable, and she could instantly see the trouble boiling beneath. He had a chip on his shoulder that almost brought him to violence several times that very night. Once they had begun verbally corresponding, he would tolerate no other boy intruding in their game of coupling. She brought these confrontations to sweet conclusions by small gestures of accommodation or words of conciliation and comfort to the participants. It was a gift she possessed: the ability to encompass more than one person in her attention at a time and make none feel the less for it.

That gift along with Josephine's other numerous attributes were what drew James to change his life for the want of her. He realized instinctively that, although she liked the danger he represented, Josephine would soon be lost to him if he did not learn to control his baser self. She was someone who wanted the hint and anticipation of contention but not the consequences of its conclusion.

He began that day to renew his life, to mold his future after a thought of how to make Josephine his own. He knew that he had to win over her father; at least to the extent that her father wouldn't be an obstacle to his future with Josie, as she liked to be called. Josie liked the notion that James was not who her father would have picked for her. She didn't want a cookie-cutter partner. She wanted a man on whom she could count day by day but who was unpredictable within that context. She wanted someone who would adventure with her and would take care of her on her adventures. She wanted someone who was not afraid to stand out, who was not afraid to defend her—to the death or to life. She wanted someone of whom others would be somewhat afraid, but not she.

She found that man in James Vanderlin, and she was soon pregnant.

This was, of course, the very thing that won over her father. He could not allow his daughter to bear a child outside of marriage. The shame of it would be even more unbearable than that normally felt by James's father. A marriage would have to take place, and James would have to find a suitable job—which, between the fathers, could be arranged.

And so James Vanderlin became a constable himself. He found this a suitable job, one that allowed him to exercise the violence that needed expression and gave him a certain power over other people. He was not a nice man as a police officer or as a human being, except to his wife and, later, to his daughter. His wife and daughter were the delight of his existence. Only in them did he find sanctuary from frustration and anger, and only with them did his life make sense.

Being a constable also brought James the opportunity to bring money to the hole behind the brick in the fireplace. He would come home at different hours of the night with stories of his ill-gotten gains, money culled from the illegal labors of others not smart enough to hide their activities from James. Josie always marveled at how her husband so easily was able to strip the largess from those miscreants. She was proud of him, and his activities brought her certain physical comforts that a constable's salary didn't afford. It was exciting to luxuriate in the secret riches for which no one was the wiser. She was convinced that, no matter what their circumstances, her husband would be able to provide whatever she needed, for there was nothing beyond his imagination and his acquiring skills.

After a time, James was promoted to more profitable positions within the constabulary. These positions expanded his sphere of influence and brought even more money to the hiding place in the fireplace. By the time his daughter Jessica was fifteen, James had expanded his enterprises to include nine squads of constables who were required but willing to bring him a percentage of their ill-gotten fortunes. He personally selected recruits to the constabulary who would be pliable to his teachings on intimidation and acquisition. He had literally formed a criminal enterprise within the constabulary of Peoria.

With the proceeds from his enterprises, James had purchased a saloon. More correctly, he had converted his father's old church into a drinking establishment that also catered to men's need for temporary female companionship. His father had died in ignorance of James's activities some months earlier, resting in his peace that James had truly become a respectable and responsible, if not Christian, member of the community. He was actually proud of his son and proclaimed his pride publicly, often citing his son's accomplishments to the astonishment of his parishioners.

Then gold was discovered in January of 1848 in California, which precipitated two-thirds of the male population of

Oregon at the time to go to California to cash in on early gold discoveries. The news spread and the next year, 1849, brought hordes of people from the east, including Europe and the Far East, to try to make their fortunes in the northern Californian gold fields. The year 1849 was the first year of large-scale cholera epidemics in America, as well as the rest of the world, and many people trying for the gold fields never made it.

This however did not deter James Vanderlin from selling his wife and daughter on the idea of cashing out their enterprises in Peoria, Illinois, and seeking their further fortunes in California. It sounded like the great adventure to Josie and Jessie, and their liquidated holdings would provide for their travel in relative comfort. When they reached California, which seemed exotic in and of itself, their current riches would launch them on to even greater wealth, especially as described by James in florid and exaggerated prose.

This is what brought them to that fateful day on the California Trail just north of the Humboldt River Valley in present-day Nevada. They had left the Oregon Trail at Fort Hall in the Idaho Territory and had journeyed south passing American Falls, Massacre Rocks, Register Rock, and Coldwater Hill. Near the junction of the Raft River and the Snake River, they had paid thirty dollars to have their wagon ferried across the Snake River by boatmen on their raft. Most of the travelers in the wagon train had to continue on down the river valley to Three Island Crossing because they could not afford the ferry. At Three Island Crossing, the wagons could cross the river because of the division in the river caused by the islands. The Snake River was swift and was made more treacherous by hidden holes in the river bottom, which caused many wagons to overturn when a wheel hit a hole, often drowning one or more of the passengers.

The Vanderlins were lucky to have the resources to pay for ferry crossings, not just on the Snake River but also previously on the Sweetwater River, the Green River, the

North Platte River, and the Laramie River all in Wyoming as well as the Missouri River and the Platte River in Nebraska. The disadvantage was that they had to wait for those other wagons that had to trek further downstream to find a portage or push on by themselves with those few who could pay as the Vanderlins did.

When James saw the rider approaching, they were moving with five other wagons toward the Humboldt River where the thirty other wagons would meet up with them, just north of present-day Wells, Nevada. As the small group of wagons had recently depleted their supply of meat, they had sent one of the wagon masters on a fresh horse to find game. It was he who was riding toward the wagons out of the sunset. James could see that the man had fulfilled his mission and was carrying the body of a small elk across his saddle. Josie and Jessie leaned over the wooden seat, peering out of the wagon to excitedly watch the man approach. They looked at each other, smiling, for there would be the wonderful smell of meat cooking over an open fire soon.

CHAPTER 5

Springfield, Illinois

Elizabeth Ryder turned from the list on the table to address her brother. Jason was at the computer desk, busily reading what was on the screen.

"What did you say?" she asked.

"I said this Vanderlin dude was a bad guy!" Jason replied, hunching over the computer keyboard, totally absorbed in the information on the screen.

Elizabeth rose from her chair and walked over to stand behind her brother in order to see the screen. "Why was he so bad?" she asked.

"Apparently, he controlled a lot of what happened in Virginia City in Nevada during the 1860s. He owned parts of gold mines, buying up the interests of the smaller claim holders when they got into trouble, and seemed to have his hand in much of what happened in the town itself. He wasn't an official of Virginia City, but he seemed to be part of what happened behind the scenes," Jason summarized. He continued reading.

"That doesn't sound so bad!" Elizabeth exclaimed. "I thought you said he was a bad guy?!"

"Listen to this!" Jason said, pointing at the screen. "'Vanderlin was thought to have been the orchestrator of one of the biggest scandals in Virginia City history when he won the rights to a third share in one of the prominent mining claims by blackmailing one of the claim holders. He operated a bordello, several saloons, and at least two mines; seemed to have been one of the organizers of the opium trade in the Virginia City/Carson City area at the time; and was generally considered to have been the perpetrator of more than one murder for profit. Yet for all of his wickedness, his name was little known outside of that locale and that time.'"

"Wow!" Elizabeth retorted. "I wonder if Dad knew any of this. He certainly would have been excited! To think we are descended from this kind of guy makes me kind of shiver!"

Jason laughed. "Yah, but every family has a James Vanderlin somewhere in the woodpile. The laws of probability certainly extend to nature and to families. Why should we be exempt?"

Elizabeth seemed lost in thought. "Let's hope it stayed with him and didn't get passed down from generation to generation."

Jason reached up and pretended to grab Elizabeth around the throat.

"Do you mean me?" he snarled laughingly.

"Stop it!" She commanded, wrestling away from him. "Does it say anything about his stepson, this Eli Wilkes?"

Jason turned back to the computer, peering at the screen.

"Not much," he responded. "Just what was printed in your magazine article a while back. He didn't get along with his stepdad and ultimately stole from him when his mother died. Apparently, he blamed his stepdad for his mother's death."

"Does it say anything about the treasure?" Elizabeth asked, walking back to her chair and picking up the list she had been working on.

"No," Jason answered. He glanced at his sister. "How is the response from your letters and your Internet advertisement?"

"Five relatives have written to say they will be there in August. A couple even sent pictures." She held up several photographs of individuals who looked older than Elizabeth and Jason. "I wonder if there will be anyone our age."

"Your age, you mean. I am significantly older and more mature than you." Jason said, grinning.

Elizabeth dismissed him with a haughty toss of her hair. "I just hope more are coming than this. I hope our family is bigger than just five relatives on Dad's side."

"What does Grandma say?"

Elizabeth stopped fiddling with the photographs and glanced out the window. A car had driven by at a high rate of speed, squealing its tires. Someone shouted at the driver angrily. The driver, a teenager, was much too young to care, and continued down the street entirely too quickly for the type of neighborhood, for any neighborhood. It was a quiet neighborhood, she pondered. Sometimes too quiet. It was almost refreshing to hear the shouts and the roaring of the miscreant vehicle with its screaming rubber and wisps of tire smoke.

Elizabeth smiled to herself, realizing that she was young for the neighborhood. Most of the people that lived on her grandmother's street were elderly, at least compared to Elizabeth and Jason. Their neighbors liked both Elizabeth and Jason because Elizabeth and Jason were respectful and seemed interested in their neighbors' conversations. This was due wholly to their grandmother and their father who insisted on these small courtesies toward others. Not that either child found it difficult to be courteous. Their personalities were such that an interest in the lives and stories of others was not feigned. As such, each child in his or her own right was very popular with both children and adults.

They just didn't seem to need anyone but each other. This had been true their entire lives since their mother had left. Each had felt abandoned in an individual way and, along with their father, had found solace in each other. It was as if they shared something, some hurt, that was indescribable to others and sometimes caused them to be solitary and morose. Their friends didn't understand them in these times and thought that something was wrong with them. But Jason and Elizabeth and their father knew that it was not a debilitating condition but simply a withdrawing into a place of healing, a place where they could look at where they were and decide if it was all right. It always was all right, they realized.

But it had hurt Elizabeth deeply when Jason went away to voluntary military service. She had felt as if part of herself was gone, was lost to her until her brother's return. It was not an overt feeling but something hidden in her that sometimes ached. It had happened again after their father died, this ache. It was why the reunion with relatives on their father's side of the family seemed so important. That was the island toward which she and Jason were floating, the place of solidness and comfort. Their grandmother never understood this need on any of their parts, the need to band together. It was what separated Jason and Elizabeth from her as it had their father before them.

Would the reunion with unknown relatives be the place of solidness and comfort? Elizabeth wondered. Or would she find it profoundly disappointing? In the end, she knew that her speculations didn't matter. She and Jason would do this, and as long as they did it together, it would be all right. Suddenly, Elizabeth realized that Jason was still waiting for her answer to his question.

"Grandma won't talk about it," she replied. "Grandma thinks the whole thing is silly. She says the stories about her great-uncle Vanderlin are unimportant and should be left as stories. I don't think she believes most of them, but he was someone the family simply didn't talk about. Unlike Dad, who loved the family dirt, Grandma finds it embarrassing and morally bankrupt."

"So I take it she is not coming with?" Jason asked.

"No. I have asked the neighbors to look in on her when we are gone. She will be all right."

"By the way," Jason remarked, "I have made reservations at the bed-and-breakfast in Elko for the week of August 15. That is the right date, isn't it?"

"It sure is," Elizabeth responded, feeling a surge of anticipation.

CHAPTER 6

The California Trail (1850)

Josie, Jessie, and James Vanderlin were standing around the elk that William Edwards had brought in, along with the thirteen others in their party. It was a small elk, not big enough to feed everyone for long. They were discussing how to divide the elk to make it last as long as possible. It had been several days since they had seen any other wild game, and Edwards, by his account, had to ride quite some distance to find this paltry example. James volunteered to Josie that he would continue to eat the hardtack that they still had so that Josie and Jessie could have fresh meat. He would not abide her protests that he was the one who should have the better nourishment as he was the man and the one who might have to protect them.

The Vanderlins had been on the trail for almost four months. They had left Peoria, Illinois, in early April of 1850 and had crossed Illinois and Missouri by stagecoach to St. Joseph, Missouri. When they reached St. Joseph in late April, James found accommodations for them in a family home where several rooms were rented to travelers such as themselves for a modest fee. Josie preferred this over a boardinghouse or an inn because the atmosphere lent itself to a family setting, where meals were taken with the family and the rooms had the feeling of warmth.

James busied himself during the following weeks securing a prairie schooner for ninety-five dollars and two oxen at forty dollars per yoke for the journey. He had found that oxen were cheaper than horses and mules and, although slower, survived better on the sparse grass reputedly found on the trail. Oxen were tamer than horses or mules and were easier to handle after they were trained. James was told that if an ox ran off at night, it was usually easier to find and catch, and the Indians along the way were less interested in stealing them.

As recommended for the length of the journey, James purchased three hundred pounds of flour, forty pounds of corn meal, fifty pounds of bacon, forty pounds of sugar, twenty pounds of coffee, thirty pounds of dried fruit, twenty pounds of salt, one pound of baking soda, four pounds of tea, ten pounds of rice, and thirty pounds of beans. He bought ten watertight barrels in which to store these foods and the water that they would find along the way. He counted on locating meat as they went along and believed, rightly, that there would be cattle traveling with them that could be purchased.

James had the barrels filled with food stored in rows in the wagon. On top of barrels was placed cotton and straw matting on which Josie and Jessie would sleep. James would likely sleep underneath the wagon or out in the open. Over the wagon was a canvas cover that was doubled and treated with linseed oil to help keep out the rain, dust, and wind—although they would discover later that it leaked rather consistently. James also bought ten chickens that were kept in crates tied to the side of the wagon. These would hopefully provide eggs and, later, meat when their egg-producing days were done.

The Vanderlins each bought three changes of clothing with four pairs of boots and four boxes of equal height to the barrels in which to store the clothing and other items. Twenty-five pounds of soap was purchased, along with a washtub and a washboard. Several blankets, pillows, and canvas ground covers were also bought as well as ink and paper and writing quills. James was able to find an excellent folding knife, some awls, scissors, pins, needles, and a variety of threads. A tin of tar was also purchased to stop leaks or repair the oxen's hooves if needed.

By the beginning of May, they were ready to begin the journey. They joined a wagon train of about eighty wagons and set off a few miles north of St. Joseph to Caples Landing, where they crossed the Missouri River. On the west side of the river, they began their trek west on the St. Joe Road. The sun was just over their morning shoulders, and they quivered with excitement. James could not stop smiling, which caused Josie to laugh out loud and pull his hat down over his nose. Jessie crawled back into the wagon in disgust. They were on their way to their promised land, and all could hear the birds distantly singing in the air.

Within two days, the wagon train encountered the Iowa, Sac, and Fox Presbyterian Mission in northeast Kansas and the nearby Great Nemaha Subagency. The mission and agency were established in 1837 when the Iowa, Sac, and Fox Indians were moved from the site of St. Joseph, Missouri, and surrounding counties to that part of Kansas. The mission was the point at which the Fort Leavenworth Road and the Iowa Point Road crossed the St. Joe Road. Many more settlers heading west joined the wagon train there, expanding the train to about one hundred and twenty wagons. A herd of cattle also joined the wagons, driven by drovers working for a rancher in Missouri. He intended to sell the cattle in California for eight times what the cattle would fetch in Kansas or Missouri.

On the road to Alcove Springs in Kansas, so much dust was kicked up by the oxen, mules, horses, and cattle that the wagons began spreading out until there were up to fifty wagons traveling abreast. Everyone wore bandanas or scarves over their faces to keep from choking on the dust. Few people rode in the wagons as it was very rough riding, and one could walk as quickly as the wagons were pulled. The otherwise quiet of the plains was disturbed by the shouts of the men pulling and hitting the animals to make them keep up a standard pace. If a wagon fell behind the pace of the train, it was left to its own devices and was at the mercy of whatever predator might come along. Safety lay in numbers, not just regarding people or animals that might prey on a wagon but also in help getting safely across rugged terrain or the various rivers and creeks.

James was immediately grateful that he had bought the oxen rather than horses or mules. The oxen pulled the wagon, which was fairly heavily laden, without effort and could keep the pace of the train with no difficulty. They were steady, and if one became difficult, James would simply climb onto its back to reinstate normalcy. Additionally, James found that this was an easy and comfortable way for him to travel, and he encouraged Josie and Jessie to take turns atop the animals when they tired of walking. They anticipated that the trip to the gold fields of California would take about one hundred and sixty days, which would entail a lot of walking.

Alcove Spring was a campsite near the Independence Crossing of the Big Blue River near present-day Blue Rapids, Kansas. Hundreds of emigrants were camped near the site waiting to cross the river when the Vanderlins' wagon train arrived. The Big Blue River was in flood stage, and the parties had to walk a little distance to the spring in order to get water that was not muddied river water. Everyone marveled at the waterfall near the spring. At one point, Jessie came running back from a trek to the spring, her buckets sloshing with spilling water, and excitedly exclaimed that the famed Donner-Reed party had stopped there on their ill-fated journey four years earlier in 1846. One of the party, Sarah

Keyes—mother-in-law of James Reed of the famous party—had died on that very spot and was buried nearby under a huge monarch oak. In addition, Jessie said with animation that the waterfall near the spring was named after another member of the Donner-Reed party, a Naomi Pike. Jessie carved her name on the ledge of the waterfall as others had done before her.

The next landmark on their journey after they had crossed the Big Blue River was New Fort Kearny, which was located on the Platte River near the present-day town of Kearny, Nebraska. It was called New Fort Kearny because it was the second fort named *Kearny*, the first being abandoned two years earlier because it was not close enough to the Oregon-California Trail. The site for the new fort had been acquired from the Pawnee Indians for two thousand dollars in trade goods, and the fort had become one of the principal stops for emigrants traveling west.

Jessie found the fort disappointing as they passed by. It was a small military station near the bank of the Platte River with walls made largely of sod cut out in large blocks and laid up in square construction. However, James and Josie were relieved as this was the first human habitation that they had seen since crossing the Missouri River almost two hundred miles back.

At Fort Kearny, James bought a cow, along with two other families, and had it butchered. Part of the meat was dried and made into hardtack, a kind of jerky that would last for weeks. Some of the meat was placed into the sealed barrels for later consumption over the next few days, and some was cooked on the spot. Otherwise, the diet was fairly monotonous with bacon, beans, and biscuits or bread being served for breakfast, lunch, and dinner. Cooking was typically done over a campfire dug into the ground and made of whatever wood they could find, buffalo chips, or sage brush. Someone usually started a fire using flint and steel and then everyone would borrow from it to begin their own fires.

The wagon train followed the Platte River across Nebraska to the North Platte River east of the present-day city of North Platte. The Platte River drains one of the most arid areas of the Great Plains, with its flow being much lower than that of comparable-length rivers in the rest of the United States. It stretches over nine hundred miles when combined with the North Platte River, with a drainage basin of over ninety thousand square miles. For much of its length, it is a wide and shallow braided stream. People on the wagon train whispered that in many places it was a mile wide but only six inches deep, and the earlier forty-niners joked that it was too thick to drink and too thin to plow. It was first named *Nebraskier*, meaning "flat water" in the Oto Indian tongue, but was ultimately called *Plate* by the French, which was their word for "flat" and is pronounced *Platte* in English. It was ceded to the United States as part of the Louisiana Purchase.

Approximately one hundred and fifty miles after the fork where the North Platte River joined the Platte River, the wagon train encountered Chimney Rock, a massive geological formation that stands almost eight hundred feet above the plain. The Vanderlins had heard about the rock since, by that time, it was famous among the travelers using the Oregon Trail and was a spectacular landmark. They then passed by Scott's Bluff, which stood on the south side of the North Platte River. A dark cloud hung over the bluffs, heightening the grandeur of the natural monument. This was soon diminished, however, when the rain came, bringing hail with it and causing a great commotion among the wagons and animals. Several of the Vanderlins' canvas ground cloths, bought in St. Joseph, were lost to the gusting winds during the storm. Again, James was grateful for the oxen, which seemed impervious to the furious storm.

A trading post had been set up near the road in view of Scott's Bluff to do business with the travelers. There, James bought two sheep from a Pawnee Indian, one of which was immediately butchered and put to good culinary use. The other was tied to the wagon and brought along for later consumption. Unfortunately, canvas could not be purchased there.

They passed Fort Laramie, a timber-stockaded fort located one or two miles above the confluence of the Laramie River with the North Platte, where James was able to find canvas to replace the ground cloths that had blown away in the rain and hailstorm at Scott's Bluff. The ground cloths became very important because the oil-treated canvas covering the wagon continued to leak no matter how much oil was put on it. During storms, the Vanderlins all huddled under the wagon on the ground cloths with more canvas tacked to the side of the wagon to keep the rain out.

The presence of the army at Fort Laramie was encouraging to the settlers as they were hearing more and more about problems with Indians in the West. From Fort Laramie, the train continued west to Red Butte, just outside present-day Casper, Wyoming, where the North Platte turned south toward Colorado. There, the wagon train had to cross the North Platte River. Mormons had established a commercial ferryboat service about eight miles downstream in 1847 and were operating four boats continuously. It cost the Vanderlins three dollars to have their wagon taken across the river on one of the ferries, and it was accomplished surprisingly quickly. Jessie received a shock when, while standing at the rail looking down into the water, she was assaulted with the scene of a woman floating by dead, having drowned when her wagon overturned while attempting to ford the river.

From Red Butte, the wagon train cut across some rather barren terrain until they finally arrived at the Sweetwater River. All were excited for they would follow this river to the Continental Divide at South Pass, which was truly the beginning of the end of their long journey. Sixty miles into the Sweetwater River Valley they encountered Independence Rock, so named because an early exploration party had spent Independence Day there in 1830. Independence Rock was a granite glacial promontory that stood one hundred and thirty feet above the river valley and was considered a halfway point to the California gold fields.

When the wagons reached South Pass in Southwestern Wyoming, the people marveled at the sight. The slope crossing the mighty Rocky Mountains was so gradual that they could scarcely believe they had actually crossed the backbone of the great barrier. They had expected something quite different, something monumental and Herculean in effort. The pass was a broad valley between the Wind River Range to the north and the Antelope Hills to the south and was like an open saddle with prairie and sagebrush allowing a broad and nearly level route between the Atlantic and Pacific watersheds. The people in the wagon train felt exultant, for it seemed now that the point of their journey was within their reach.

The trail passed along the Bear River, splitting into three segments at Soda Springs. The mineral springs in the area were acclaimed by all travelers, and bathing in the springs brought a wanted relief from the weeks of difficult traveling. James laughed as Josie and Jessie proclaimed the virtues of the water and pushed him into the springs when he knelt down to test the temperature.

There, much to the surprise of the travelers, they saw a white woman encamped with a group of Canadian Indians. She had blue eyes and light hair, which contrasted sharply to the features of those with whom she traveled and caused the men of the wagon train to call the group into question. The woman, to their astonishment, assured them that her style of living was a matter of choice. Her husband was a French-and-Indian half blood who had pursued the Indian life, and her love for him had caused her to abandon all and follow him for the past twenty years.

The wagons reached a trading post named Fort Hall at the bottom of the Snake River in the middle of another storm. Once again, Josie and Jessie had to huddle with James under the wagon, encircled by the canvas covers and covered in thick blankets near the buildings of the trading post owned by the

Hudson's Bay Company. When the rain stopped, they bought more linseed oil at the post in another futile attempt to correct the leaks of the wagon cover. From Fort Hall, the emigrants headed west along the Snake River until they reached the Raft River and the City of Rocks geological formation. This is where the Vanderlins and five other wagons were able to cross the Snake River by ferry. The rest of the wagon train continued further down the river looking for a usable ford.

The small party, including the Vanderlins, crossed Granite Pass and were shocked, having gradually ascended to the pass, to face the rugged descent on the other side down to Goose Creek. One of the wagons broke an axle, and the party had to stop to cut wood to replace the axle. Not far from Goose Creek, the settlers entered the low hills that separate the Great Basin from the Snake River drainage and traveled southwest through the Thousand Springs Valley toward the Humboldt River. Their food stores were becoming depleted of meat, and the party decided to send William Edwards on a horse to find and bring back game. Edwards had been gone several days, and the party began worrying that something had happened to him or that he had somehow missed them on the trail. It was with great relief that they spotted him coming over the rise that fateful day.

CHAPTER 7

Elko, Nevada (Present Day)

Elizabeth and Jason stepped down from the Amtrak train and onto the platform in Elko. It was almost midnight. The platform was a simple cement surface several hundred feet long with a glass and metal open-sided shelter in the center. The edge of the platform opposite the tracks was fenced with a chain-link fence the entire length of the platform. There were no buildings on their side of the tracks, but a dirt road led up the slope to a street overpass above the railroad tracks. The other end of the dirt road seemed to follow the railroad tracks for a ways in the direction from which they had come and then disappeared into some large trucking or equipment sheds. Beyond the sheds were mostly empty juniper-dotted hills.

They looked around puzzled, disappointed. Across the tracks was a dirt-and-asphalt street that catered to several industrial businesses and a bowling alley. The street seemed to end at the bowling alley, after which there was a field of perhaps a quarter mile filled with tumbleweed-type brush. In the distance, other industrial-style businesses could be seen on the flat and at the top of a ridge. The entire area looked either blue-collar or desolate, depending on where your eyes rested, Elizabeth thought aloud.

"What?" Jason asked without looking at her, taking in their surroundings.

"How horrible!" Elizabeth exclaimed with a bit of panic in her voice. "How do we get out of here? There is nothing, no one, here!"

"It'll be all right, Sis," Jason said reassuringly. "We can cross the tracks and go over to that bowling alley. Surely they will have a phone or know of a cab service or something."

"I have my cell phone," Elizabeth responded, searching in her purse.

"Don't bother," Jason replied resignedly. "I already tried mine—no reception!"

"What about our bags?" Elizabeth's large suitcase had wheels on it, but it was quickly apparent to her that it would be a monumental task to get it over the railroad tracks to a place where the wheels would be useful. Jason's bag, although equally equipped, was not much smaller.

"We're just going to have to wrestle them over the tracks. We can't leave them here, and I am not willing to leave you here with them while I go to the bowling alley!"

"You are damned right you are not leaving me here!" Elizabeth breathed, shuddering as she glanced around. "Even if you have to carry me over with the bags, I'm going with you! God only knows what might be lurking out there!"

They struggled across the railroad tracks with Jason making two trips to get their suitcases safely across. That platform was a duplicate of the one on which they had alight from the train, so they had to walk to the end of the fence on that side of the tracks to reach the street. The bowling alley was just across the street and across a parking lot from the platform and was readying to close as they entered. Jason was able to secure a phone book and a telephone and managed to find a taxi service that would take them to the bed-and-breakfast.

The bed-and-breakfast house on Silver Street was a three-story stick-built structure that was sided, as were all of the houses on that street, in broad light-colored boards. It had a shingle roof that contained several gables, one of which hung out over the side of the house. Lights from a basement room glowed out into the dark as they arrived, which Jason perceived to be the room of the owner of the house since he had called there from the bowling alley to make certain he and Elizabeth could get in at that hour. A middle-aged man with thinning brown hair met them at the door as they were about to ring the bell. He forced a smile and touched a finger to his lips to plead for quiet and then pointed up as if to silently explain that others were sleeping. Jason and Elizabeth nodded and followed him into the house and through a door to the basement.

"I'm Vincent Lowler," the man explained in a low voice. "Welcome to the historic Silver Street Bed-and-Breakfast. Your rooms are on the top floor. I hope you don't mind, but you are among some of the youngest here right now, and we don't have elevators, so I put some of the older people on the lower floors." He whispered this in a stream of words.

When they reached Vincent's apartment in the basement, which appeared to take up most of the space, he motioned them to the kitchen table to sit in the chairs there. Jason and Elizabeth did as beckoned. Vincent sat across from them and handed them the forms to be filled out indicating the length of their stay, home addresses, phone numbers, vehicles and their license numbers, and such. He ran Jason's credit card through a machine and handed Jason a credit card form to be signed. He then gave Jason and Elizabeth keys to their rooms and again indicated they were on the top floor. Vincent volunteered to help Elizabeth carry her luggage up to her room, which she declined.

Elizabeth's room was opposite Jason's at the top of the narrow winding staircase. It seemed like they had climbed forever, dragging their suitcases behind them but trying not to allow the wheels to touch the stairs for fear of noise. The hallway at the top of the stairs was wider but still narrow by comparison with a modern hotel. In spite of the effort to get to their rooms, Elizabeth was enthralled with the atmosphere of the home. It had all of the charm of a true Victorian home: from its novel wallpaper of climbing vines and flowers to the polished carved wood of the banisters and doorjambs. The doors to their rooms were solid wood, paneled in quarter pieces that were carved with pictures of animals such as deer and bear.

Elizabeth opened the door to her room and searched in the darkness for the light switch. It was a round knob to the left of the doorjamb which, when turned, lighted two large lamps on either side of a single high, sumptuous bed. The bed had thick head—and footboards, again of carved, darkly stained wood. How glorious, she thought to herself, smiling. The lamps, encased in rich amber-beaded silk shades, stood atop tall tables of ornately chiseled mahogany. The surfaces of the tables were pink veined marble.

The room was equally magnificent. The walls were encased in light green wallpaper filled with swirls and flowers in subtle pastels of pink, brown, and blue. A dormer opened out opposite the bed onto a window above a built-in bench or cabinet seat and extended from the top of the ceiling to the corded blue cushions on the seat. The dormer was bordered by stained wood. Elizabeth could see the branches and the outline of a large oak tree outside the window in the darkness. A large, tall dresser stood against the far wall with spacious drawers that were gilded in sculptured wood of a slightly darker color than the drawers. An oversized mahogany wardrobe was placed in the corner to the left of the door and angled to face the center of the room.

Elizabeth rolled her bag into the room and then stepped back into the hall to look into Jason's room. Jason was bouncing on his bed, a bed similar to hers in accommodation and adornment. His room was as festive in color and furniture and also had a dormer that looked out over the yard on the other side of the house. A light could be seen dancing in a window of the home next door, and Elizabeth realized that that home was some distance away as the dancing of the light was caused by the swaying of numerous tree branches.

"Jason, you know there are probably other people on this floor!" Elizabeth admonished. "Bouncing on the bed at this hour, or at any hour actually, is disrespectful to the others that are sleeping!"

"You are right, as usual," Jason admitted, lying back and allowing the bed to stop shaking on its own. "What do you think? How is your room?"

"It's beautiful! Like something out of the past. It's like going back in time! I think this is going to be a great adventure!" She could feel her face brighten as she said this, but she couldn't help it. This was going to be a great adventure, even if it only meant meeting people with whom she had a tenuous connection.

"Just don't go cowboy on me," Jason teased. "I don't want to get off the train in Springfield with a sister wearing shitkickers and a big belt buckle. We would have to sell Grandma's house and move."

"I am going to bed!" Elizabeth grunted, feigning indignation. Then she added, "You didn't notice if there is a bathroom on this floor did you?"

"It looks like there is one at the end of the hall," Jason responded helpfully.

CHAPTER 8

Humboldt River Valley (1850)

          Both Josie and Jessie were sick, as were most of the women and children in the five wagons of James's abbreviated wagon train. Several of the men were sick as well. William Edwards had gone out again on the horse in search of more game and better water. He had left that morning. The women of the train had been sick since the middle of the night two nights previous, and all were concerned that they had contracted cholera from one of the infrequent water holes that they had encountered. The fear was palatable for all had seen numerous fellow travelers succumb to the perils of cholera since leaving St. Joseph, and one of the symptoms, exhaustive diarrhea, was pointedly present. However, all of the patients had been vomiting as well, and that didn't seem as indicative of cholera.

  At around four o'clock the next morning, Josie died. James was sitting between his wife and daughter as they lay prone on the mattresses inside the wagon. He sat with his head in his hands, dozing and waking to replace the wet cloths that he had placed on their foreheads. Both Josie and Jessie had fevers that racked their bodies, causing them to twist in pain and then shiver uncontrollably. James had been dozing for mere moments when he felt the death rattle of Josephine, his wife and constant companion of sixteen years. He jumped to his knees and curled her in his arms, his wails piercing the night air. He hugged her to him ardently in an insane effort to stave off the last throes of her life, as if his efforts to keep the death rattle from completing its course might save her.

He lay next to her, sobbing until she became cold to the touch of his body. He still held her through the night, not daring to let her go, not wanting to face the lifelessness of her. His mind could not comprehend how this could have happened. It was not possible! He had done everything to ensure that this did not happen! All of the meticulous planning and preparation up to this point had been done to insure that this did not happen. It was not fair—it could not be fair! There must be a reason that this happened; someone must be to blame! But who? Certainly not James! He had done everything possible to provide for every contingency. He had no real belief in God, or he would have been desperately negotiating for his wife's life. He could do nothing but cry and feel the utter hopelessness of his life without Josie.

Finally, in the morning, he stirred from his stupor and glanced at his daughter. Jessie was dead as well. She lay there, one eye closed and one eye slightly open, fixed, staring at nothing. Her skin had lost any luster of life and seemed somehow glassy, opaque, and sallow. James stared at her, still holding Josie to him. He stared at Jessie uncomprehendingly. His mind entered a fugue state and stayed that way for the rest of the day until the evening when Ben Bennett came to James's wagon to inquire about their condition. Slowly, James's mind took in the image of Ben standing against the evening sun, holding the flap of the canvas open and staring into the wagon. Ben was saying something.

"I'm sorry, James," Ben was uttering somberly. "Your women are not the only ones dead or dying! I think you and I are the only ones not touched by this evil. Three others beside Josie and Jessie have died, and I think two more may die before morning. William has not come back yet, and I fear he may not. He mentioned before he left that it might have been the meat that he brought back. When I asked what he meant, he simply said he found the elk already dead. He didn't know how long it had been dead, but I think it had turned. I don't believe this is cholera."

James did not respond, and Ben finally went away, allowing the canvas flap to fall back into place. James stayed in the wagon as Ben Bennett had left him for the rest of the day, that night, and the next day. He didn't eat or drink water, and when Ben and Willard Bradley came to the Vanderlins' wagon that second night, James was still holding Josie in the same position as Ben had previously seen him. James's eyes were hollow, and his skin looked yellow in the pale light.

"James!" Ben Bennett commanded. "We've got to get your women into the ground before they turn! Come on, man! You've got to help us here!"

Light and recognition came back into James's eyes, and he looked around as if he didn't know where he was. Then he lay Josie back down on the mattress and crawled forward, stepping down from the wagon. He stared up at the sky for a second and then glanced at the scene in front of him. There was freshly piled dirt in five rows, two of them child size, in the circle between the wagons, and two holes in the ground lay open next to the last pile. He glared at the gaping holes for a moment and then walked off between the wagons into the dusk. Ben Bennett and Willard Bradley looked at each other in confusion.

"What's he doin'?" Willard asked, bewildered.

"Let's just go ahead and plant 'em," suggested Ben Bennett.

And that is what they did. James Vanderlin came back to the camp close to the morning. He had wandered aimlessly during the darkness, although never far from the circle of wagons subtly lit by the glow of the campfires. He had never stopped walking in and around the sagebrush and yucca trees throughout the night, whispering to himself and gesturing wildly at times. By the time he reentered the camp, he was ragged and drawn. He crawled back into his wagon and immediately passed out, exhausted, not seeming to notice the absence of his wife and daughter.

It was noon before James stirred from his wagon. The other wagons were tidying up, preparing to leave. Randall Whitehouse was pounding the last of seven crosses into the ground above the mounds of overturned earth. On each cross was carved the name of the person who lay beneath and the date of the dying. James stared fixedly at the two crosses bearing the names of Josie and Jessie. As if he had come to a resolution, he turned and walked to the wagon of Jasper Farley. Jasper was bridling his horse to tie to the back of his old wood-warped farm wagon. The wagon had been overloaded during the early part of the journey with bits of used furniture and belongings, much of which had been discarded during the trek from St. Joseph. The wagon was now sparely loaded with only the essentials with which Jasper and his wife Sarah deemed they could not part. One of the graves belonged to their young son Virgil who had preceded Josie in death. Everyone, with the exception of James and Ben Bennett—both of whom had not eaten any of the elk—had been stricken with the sickness. All but those lying in the seven graves had recovered.

"I'll trade you my oxen and wagon and everything in it for your horse," James said to Jasper without any emotion. He said this as if he were discussing the weather. Jasper just stared at him for some moments.

"I'm sorry," he responded incredulously. "Did you say you wanted to trade all of your belongings for my horse?"

James nodded. He still didn't make eye contact with Jasper but looked off into the distance without seeing what was there.

"But what about all of your things? What will you do without your things?" Jasper asked.

"I just need a horse!" James exclaimed with more force. "I don't want the rest. I can't be around it! The oxen will outpull your mangy mules, and your wagon won't likely make it to California, especially with the road ahead. I'm offering you my oxen and wagon with all of the stuff in it for your horse! I will take what I need from the wagon, but I need a horse and saddle. Do you agree?"

"Yes, I will trade you my horse for your oxen and wagon." Jasper sighed. "I must say that I think you are making a mistake. But then the mistake is yours to make, so I will agree to the trade."

James went back to his wagon and rifled under the seat for the box containing the money that he and Josie had spent years accumulating. He emptied the box into a leather satchel and picked up the rifle and several boxes of bullets that lay next to the box. He put the bullets into the satchel as well. He crawled back into the wagon, opened one of the boxes, and removed several items of clothing, his hat, and an overcoat. He rolled the clothes into the overcoat and tied it with a piece of rope. He grabbed two blankets, rolled the overcoat in the blankets, and tied it again with another piece of rope. He pulled some biscuits, bacon, and hardtack out of the barrels; put them in another leather bag; and scooped water from another barrel into a canteen. He then left the wagon and walked over to Jasper who was saddling the horse.

James mounted the horse as Jasper stepped back, discouraged, and rode it to where Ben Bennett was standing watching them.

"Which way did William Edwards ride?" James asked—rather, commanded.

Ben Bennett pointed to the west and then asked, "What are you doin', James?"

James Vanderlin spurred the horse to the west, charging immediately into a gallop.

"Don't go doin' somthin' foolish!" Jasper shouted after him.

Jasper's admonition was lost on the wind as James rode away across the heather toward the hill to the west. His figure slowly diminished over the hill as all of those left in the wagon party watched, astounded. It was the last time they would ever see James Vanderlin.

CHAPTER 9

Elko, Nevada (Present Day)

Elizabeth opened the bathroom door at the bed-and-breakfast on Silver Street. She walked down the hall to her room in her bathrobe and slippers. It was cool in the house, and the terrycloth bathrobe felt nice and warm. Jason was waiting in her room, completely dressed and stretched out across her already-made bed. He had his hands clasped behind his head and was looking up at the sculptured plaster of the ceiling.

"Out!" she commanded. "I have to get dressed!"

He stretched and moved languidly as if he were drugged.

"Come on, Jason! Let me get dressed, or I will miss breakfast!" She threw her towel at his face, missing by inches.

He moved more quickly now to his own room across the hall. His bed was, as usual, unmade. His suitcase was on a suitcase-collapsible stand against the wall by the wardrobe with clothes piled into the suitcase helter-skelter. Elizabeth, on the other hand, had made her bed, hung her hanging clothes in the wardrobe, and placed her folding clothes in the dresser. Her suitcase was standing closed next to the wardrobe, out of the way. Her cosmetics and dressing implements—brushes, hair clasps, spongies, and purse items—were neatly organized on the small table on the other side of the wardrobe from her suitcase.

Elizabeth dressed in a fairly short time in a pair of tan slacks, a maroon blouse, and dark brown slip-on shoes accented by light maroon socks. Her long blond hair had been sufficiently combed to reflect the personal care she took in her appearance. She wore very little makeup, nothing more than some eyeliner and dark red lipstick. She gathered up the items in her purse that were needed or not to be left in the room and proceeded to her brother's room. He was lying on his own bed this time in the same configuration as he had been on hers. He was dressed in blue jeans and a brown tee shirt with black tennis shoes over white crew socks. She looked at him from the doorway somewhat critically but said nothing in that vein. He was her brother, and although she would have preferred that he make a better first impression on those that they would meet by his appearance, she knew the futility of any such suggestion.

"I'm ready," she announced. He looked at her appraisingly for a moment and then sat up swinging his legs to the floor.

"And away we go!" he commented, passing her in the hallway.

The stairway to the first floor turned four times before they descended into the hallway that led to the outside of the house in either direction. As they looked down into the first floor hallway from the last landing, they could see that there were several doors that opened onto the hallway, including the door that led to Vincent Lowler's basement apartment. The doors nearest the front of the house stood open, and as Elizabeth and Jason descended the stairs, they could look into the rooms. There were people milling about in the second room from the front of the house and, by the sounds emanating from that room, the siblings guessed that was where breakfast was being served.

The dining room was festooned in light blue wallpaper between large windows dressed in dark blue curtains. There was a large table in the center of the room made of darkly stained oak, surrounded by a dozen chairs that were descriptive of the last century in their construction. To the window side of the great table was a smaller oval-shaped wooden table grounded by two spindle-style carved legs with flayed feet. Atop this table was displayed a variety of cold foods including bagels, cookies of different makes and shapes, various pastries, a bin of cream cheese and another of strawberry jelly, a coffee urn and cups, saucers, and small plates. There were utensils in the bins to assist in their utility.

Five people were gathered in the room, including Vincent Lowler. Vincent hurried to Elizabeth and Jason, drawing them into the room.

"Folks, may I have your attention?" He postured grandly. "Our newest arrivals are Jason and Elizabeth Ryder, here from Springfield, Illinois. Please introduce yourselves to them and make them welcome!" Turning back to Elizabeth and Jason, he continued, "There is food on the side table and coffee as well. Please help yourselves."

An older lady of perhaps seventy years of age moved toward them as Jason and Elizabeth edged toward the food table. She held out her hand as she approached them.

"At last I get to meet you face to face," she said, grabbing Elizabeth's hand. She was a medium-sized woman, perhaps five feet four inches in height, with gray hair that was cut short; she was somewhat stocky in stature. Her grip was stout and her voice strong. She was dressed in a conservative gray two-piece pant suit with a white blouse and black, tied, flat shoes with a closed toe.

"My name is Isadora Dulles, 'Izzy' for short, and that is my son, Benjamin," she said, pointing to a small middle-aged man with an almost bald pate who was talking to a taller gentleman of about the same age. "It is actually my son that you have been corresponding with, but I was thrilled that two such young people would be so interested in history and particularly our family history. We would never have done this if it weren't for you getting hold of everyone! It is simply marvelous!"

Elizabeth reddened with embarrassment and turned to Jason for silent support. Izzy was still shaking her hand and didn't seem in a hurry to let go.

"It was really nothing!" Elizabeth said modestly. "This is my brother Jason. He was the one who found everyone on the Internet. I would never have known how to do it otherwise."

Izzy turned her gaze to Jason approvingly. "Umm," she said provocatively, as only an older lady could do, inspiring glee rather than offense, at least in Elizabeth. Jason colored much brighter than his sister and shook Izzy's hand lightly, as if too long a touch would somehow contaminate. Izzy turned back to Elizabeth, instinctively knowing which sibling was the narrator of the events that brought them all together.

She began acquainting Elizabeth with those in the room in a quiet, conspiratorial way, almost whispering as she spoke. The man talking to her son was an accountant from Van Nuys, California, named Ed Walch. He was here with his cousin Andy, also a Walch, who was standing nearest the window and eating a pastry directly from the side table. The Walch cousins had arrived just before Izzy and her son the previous day. Izzy wasn't sure of Andy Walch's profession other than that he dealt with children. Both Walches were unmarried: Andy having never married and Ed being recently, within the last two years, divorced. Additionally, Ed seemed to have four children in various stages of adulthood that he supported in some fashion.

The couple sitting at the end of the large table eating bagels and creamed cheese was Marjorie and Marvin Cosgrove. Marjorie was the descendant of the Vanderlin family, not her husband. They operated some type of transportation service in Renton, Washington, and by the look of them, were in their middle to late forties. They had one child, a son who was at Washington State University studying biology. They were very proud that he wanted to become a doctor but were unsure how they would be able to finance medical school.

Izzy concluded the informal introductions with herself and her son. Until her retirement some five years before, Izzy had worked as a teacher at a reform school in Grand Rapids, Michigan. She had a decent pension that allowed her to enjoy these kinds of trips with her son. Benjamin Dulles was a fifty-four-year-old ne'er-do-well (not Izzy's assessment) antiques dealer who operated a small business out of his mother's garage and could only travel at the largess of his doting mother. He was fascinated by historical oddities and was particularly interested in his illustrious ancestor James Vanderlin, whom he had industriously studied. On one of their vacation trips, Izzy had taken Benjamin to Virginia City, Nevada, to visit the final resting place of James Vanderlin.

"Are you interested in James Vanderlin?" Izzy asked Elizabeth and Jason.

Elizabeth laughed.

"Not really," she admitted. "We recently lost our father, who was an only child, so we don't have any direct relatives on his side of the family. Our mom left when we were young, and we don't know much about her side." Elizabeth blushed slightly, wondering if she was disclosing too much personal information. She glanced at Jason for any hint of guidance, but he gave no indication that she had gone too far. He seemed simply interested in her explanation.

Noticing her discomfort, Jason added, "What Liz is trying to say is that we don't know much about Vanderlin. We are more interested in meeting some of Dad's relatives and so Liz came up with this idea."

Elizabeth picked up the flow. "I read about James Vanderlin in our Sunday paper and thought it would be a good excuse for a kind of family reunion. The treasure hunt idea seemed like it might encourage more people to come. Jason was the one who figured out how to find people on the Internet, but I was the one who wrote the letters."

"Um," Izzy said pensively. "So you don't believe the treasure exists?"

Both Elizabeth and Jason laughed. "We don't know," Jason commented. "We don't really care. If everyone really wants to look for it, we will help, but we don't care one way or the other."

"I thought it would be a fun way to get to know people, that's all," Elizabeth added.

"Well that is a relief!" Izzy exhaled. "I was afraid you might be like my son, obsessed with a ghost. He was so excited when I agreed to sponsor this trip that I thought he might have a heart attack. He knows all about this house and its history, although he has never had a chance to stay here. I offered a vacation to the Bahamas, but he would have none of it. Not after getting your letter."

"I am glad you did this instead," Elizabeth said sincerely. "And I can't wait to talk to your son. Jason tried to find out about James Vanderlin on the Internet, but there isn't much there. Maybe Benjamin will be able to tell us more about him."

"Of that you can be certain!" Izzy laughed.

CHAPTER 10

Humboldt Wells, Utah Territory (1850)

James Vanderlin crouched atop the ridge overlooking the valley below. Lush meadows and clear springs made the place a natural rest stop for the emigrants on their way to California. Those pioneers preceding the Vanderlins' wagon train called it Humboldt Wells. It was the beginning of a tough and deadly journey over four hundred miles of barren high desert. Its springs and swampy area were the source of the Humboldt River along which the travelers would journey through the desert until finally reaching the Sierra Nevada Mountains. This was the spot where James and the other wagons that had afforded ferrying were to meet the rest of the wagon train that had to find portage downstream on the Snake River. The wagons from the main body of the train had yet to arrive, as had the wagons from James's group.

From the top of the ridge, James could see the glow of a campfire becoming visible in the valley below as the sun crept down behind the mountains to the west. He sat there hunched down on his legs, resting on his feet for at least an hour until the dusk had settled sufficiently. There was no doubt in James's mind who sat before that fire, stoking it to bring the flames higher. He had followed William Edwards to this place, not so much tracking him as knowing that this was where he would go. James had pushed his horse to get here, barely stopping to rest, eat, or drink water. His horse was exhausted, as was James. Yet he could not stop now. He was close to the source of his rage.

Just before darkness fell, James tied his horse to a bramble bush on the other side of the small ridge from the campfire. He took the rifle from the saddle and began making his way down the hill toward the fire. The sun had set on the other side of the valley, so James was confident he would not be silhouetted against the darkened sky behind him. What little light remained before the night truly fell was before him and was needed to negotiate the distance down the hill without falling prey to some hidden obstacle. He couldn't afford to alert Edwards by some noisy stumble on his part, for surprise was essential in this task. He wanted Edwards completely at his mercy. He wanted to see the fear in Edwards's eyes and to see that Edwards knew what awaited him.

The matter resolved as James had wished it. He silently stepped into the light of the fire while Edwards stooped over a pan held near the fire. William Edwards was wearing the guilt of his accomplishments on his person. His clothes were rumpled, dusty, and unkempt. His face had a haggard look, and his hair was bedraggled and filthy. It wasn't just that he had ridden hard—certainly not as hard as James to catch up to him. He had stopped caring for his appearance, for anything except flight. He had resignation and culpability draped over his body like a cloak. Even so, James didn't need to confirm the sin by seeing it so plainly before him. He knew what he would do deep in his mind from the moment Ben Bennett had told him of his suspicions. James needed no proof beyond what he believed to be true.

James stood silently at the edge of the firelight, the rifle pointed directly at William Edwards. Edwards, sensing something, looked up, looked into James's eyes as if drawn there by some immutable force. His face fell in its expression of surprise, and his eyes registered the finality of his plight. He could see in James's eyes the futility of any protest. He was caught by the devil of death, and there was no one to mitigate for him. He stood and instinctively drew the figure of the cross across his body. He began to say something, something of regret, when the bullet from James's rifle struck him in the chest. The sound of the rifle did not register in William's consciousness, but the force of the projectile propelled him backward and onto a patch of rabbit brush. He slid to the ground as James walked up and shot him in the face.

James walked back to the fire and picked up the pan that William had dropped. There was still some food clinging to the bottom, beans and rice by appearance. James lay down his rifle on the saddle no longer needed by William and scooped the food from the pan into his mouth with his fingers. It tasted good, and James had not eaten anything but hardtack in a day and a half. He didn't look at the prone, sprawled figure of the dead William Edwards. He stood with his back to the body, not acknowledging its presence, and ate Edwards's food. After finishing the last of the beans and rice and two biscuits that had been set to the side of the fire, James strode back up the hill as best he could in the dark and retrieved his horse. He brought the horse down to the firelight and hobbled it next to William Edwards's horse. He then lay down on William Edwards's bedroll blanket and fell fast asleep.

When he awoke the next morning, the first image to enter James's eyes was the dead form of William Edwards lying still against the rabbit brush. His face was unrecognizable due to the gaping hole from the last bullet fired from James's rifle the night before. James turned away from what used to be William Edwards and stoked the embers of the previous night's fire. There was enough heat left to get the fire going again with little effort. James rummaged through Edwards's belongings and found more biscuits and some bacon, which he cooked and ate.

For the first time since Josie and Jessie came into his life, James had to consider what his life was going to be like without them. Since their untimely demise, he had been consumed with blame and exacting justice on he whom James blamed. He had imagined with intense hatred the recent events leading to the former William Edwards lying exactly as he lay. He had not imagined anything after that. Now, as he sat drinking the last of the made coffee, he would have to consider what was next. Should he leave William Edwards as he was, allowing the body to putrefy and to be eaten and carried off by scavengers? Should he bury him? And if so, where? Did he care whether anyone found Edwards?

At this time James did not have a mark against his name—not publicly, anyway. Ben Bennett and those with him would know that James had gone looking for Edwards, and if they found him destroyed by rifle bullets, James would certainly be blamed. If Edwards were never found, they would still interpret that James had found him. But they wouldn't be able to prove anything. Rumor was not the same thing as proof. James could live with rumor; indeed, he cared nothing about it. However, he did not want to become a hunted man at this time. He needed time to figure out what he would do from here.

And so James wrapped the body of William Edwards in Edwards's blanket and, after saddling Edwards's horse, put him across the saddle. James picked up all that he could find that would have shown that Edwards had been there, wrapped that up in some of Edwards's clothing, and tied that across the saddle as well. He saddled his own horse, climbed up into the saddle, and rode southeast followed by Edwards on his horse. He rode southeast that entire day until he found a gully, more of a gash in a hill, and rolled Edwards's body off of the horse and down into the gully. By the time James had resecured Edwards's horse to his own, vultures had already begun circling above the gully. It would only be a matter of time before William Edwards would only be a distant memory in the minds of his fellow travelers, with no one being able to prove that misfortune had befallen him. The place of Edwards's bereavement was sufficiently off any trail used by settlers that it would be unlikely for his body to be found.

James then camped for the night nearby and, in the morning, swung his horse, along with Edwards's horse, westward.

CHAPTER 11

Elko, Nevada (Present Day)

Elizabeth stood in the center of the room looking at the painting on the wall. She was standing in the drawing room of the bed-and-breakfast house on Silver Street. A train whistle could be heard not that distant away. She cocked her head to the side slightly as she stared at the picture and tried to visualize the room from Eli Wilkes's perspective. What was he looking at? she wondered. His eyes were sad, but his carriage was erect and proud, almost defiant. Was he only seeing the person painting the picture, or did he perceive something more? She thought his expression communicated something: but what?

The room in the picture looked very like the one she was standing in now. The wallpaper was slightly different in pattern, but the color was very similar. It must have been difficult for Vincent Lowler to recreate the setting of the original painting in the room of today. The old style wallpaper must have been very difficult to obtain, even though it differed slightly from that in the painting. The settee under the painting was almost identical to that in the painting—similar fabric, same colors, and same style pattern in the upholstery. It must have cost a bundle to renovate in this way, Elizabeth pondered.

Elizabeth looked about the rest of the room and thought about the parts that were not exhibited in the painting. Were the tables and chairs the same as those of over one hundred years ago? She wondered what Lowler based the renovation of the rest of the house on: the kitchen, the bedrooms, the bathrooms, and the hallways. Did he have other pictures of the house from the time of Eli Wilkes to establish the decorations of the rooms, or was it done simply according to his imagination?

Izzy Dulles and her son Benjamin had stepped into the room.

"It's delightful, isn't it?" commented Izzy on Elizabeth's obvious scrutiny of the room. "I think Vincent has done a marvelous job at recreating a nineteenth-century drawing room. Don't you think so, Bennie?"

It was clear that Izzy was trying to bring her son, whom she obviously thought was socially inept, into a dialogue with Elizabeth, who seemed to her more urbane.

"Yes, mother," Benjamin answered with little enthusiasm.

Elizabeth immediately picked up on Izzy's intent.

"Would you happen to know if Mr. Lowler used actual photographs or pictures to renovate the rest of the house?" she directed the question to Benjamin.

"I don't know," answered Benjamin, looking around at the room critically, probably for the first time. "It looks authentic enough. I have read books and seen pictures of the time period, and this seems pretty consistent with what I have seen and read."

His eyes stopped at the painting of Eli Wilkes. He stroked his chin with his fingers as he studied the picture.

"You know, the theory is that the clues to find old Vanderlin's gold is in this picture," he commented abstractly, as if talking to himself. "I've seen pictures of this painting in magazines and books, but this is the first time I have actually looked at it. It is much smaller than I imagined. They have never been able to find the two pictures that were on either side of Eli Wilkes in the painting."

He moved closer to the painting, studying it more severely.

"Umm," he said mysteriously.

Elizabeth and Izzy moved closer to the painting as well. The two pictures on either side of Eli Wilkes were presented in the background of the painting, establishing the distance of Eli Wilkes from the wall of the salon. They were paintings of two women, one woman obviously older than the other but wearing fashions that were contemporary to each other and perhaps of a time earlier than that worn by Eli Wilkes. The women were unremarkable in their appearance except that both seemed to radiate happiness in their expression and their eyes. Perhaps they were employees of the brothel, thought Elizabeth, or loved ones of employees of the brothel. Or perhaps they were from a different time than the brothel's time. That would probably make more sense since Elizabeth could not imagine a great deal of happiness coming out of working in a brothel.

"Perhaps the owners of the paintings took them with them when they left," Elizabeth suggested, then changing the focus: "Why would Eli Wilkes have had a self-portrait done if he knew he was going to die?"

Benjamin Dulles looked at Elizabeth more directly this time. "That's an interesting question," he said. "There are two theories. One is that he knew he was going to be killed and wanted to leave something behind to be remembered by."

Izzy laughed. "It seemed to work. It is over a hundred years later and we are still talking about him."

"What is the other theory?" Elizabeth asked as Jason and Vincent Lowler walked through the door to the salon and noticed them.

"Just what I mentioned before," said Benjamin. "That somewhere in this painting is the clue to the whereabouts of the treasure of James Vanderlin."

"I doubt that," responded Vincent Lowler, his expression reflecting his words. "I have spent quite some time with that picture, and I have never seen anything amounting to a clue to anything. I think it is exactly what it appears to be—a picture of a guy who knows that he will soon be dead. Everybody looks at that painting and overanalyzes it. I think his 'sad' expression is due to the fact that he knows he is going to be killed. It was why he stopped running and stayed here. He was tired and knew that they would catch him sooner or later. His stepfather was rich enough to have him followed until they caught him, and he knew it. He had the picture painted to leave something behind."

"Do you believe there is a treasure?" Jason intervened.

Both Vincent and Benjamin responded at the same time.

"No," was Vincent's reply.

"Of course there is a treasure!" came Benjamin. "Why else would James Vanderlin send killers after Eli Wilkes if it wasn't to get back what belonged to him?"

Elizabeth continued to be puzzled.

"How do we know that Vanderlin didn't get back all that belonged to him?" she asked. "Maybe the killers found the treasure and brought it back to him. Or maybe they found the treasure but claimed to Vanderlin that they didn't! How do we know?"

"Exactly!" said both Jason and Vincent.

"I don't think so," replied Benjamin animatedly. "The legend exists! Legends almost always exist because they are based on fact. Look at the legend of Troy. For years it was thought to be just a story. But then they discovered that Troy actually existed! The legend is that James Vanderlin was inconsolable when the killers came back to report Eli's murder. He went into a rage! Why would he go into a rage when told of Eli's murder? After all, he had ordered it himself! Obviously because he didn't get what he wanted! The legend is that Eli stole Vanderlin's gold. The legend states that the killers only brought back a gold watch, which was all that they could find on Eli when they murdered him. After getting the gold watch back, Vanderlin went into a rage! Why? Obviously because the gold watch was not all of the treasure!"

Izzy watched the interchange with amusement. She was proud of Benjamin for his stand. He was more animated than she had seen him in months. Perhaps this trip was exactly what was needed to bring him back to life and to energy. He had been so depressed recently, as if he was finally realizing the futility of his previous life living off the charity of his mother. His antiques business out of her garage had dropped off until it was rare that anyone came by with interest in those bits and pieces that he collected. She could see his demeanor change within that last year to a kind of listless abandonment.

Benjamin Dulles had never been able to complete the life cycle that others expected of their existence. He was interested in odd things, mostly historical things, but of no particular pattern that would focus his attention. It was unpredictable what would catch his notice and his energy, but it was predictable that few others would have the same interest. As such, it was difficult for him to find others with common interests that followed a theme. Indeed, he followed no theme in his interests. He would focus on one thing for a short time or for an excruciatingly long time, but his focus would be so narrow that no one else could relate to him.

This drove Izzy to distraction for, although she could see the result, she could do nothing about it. People found Benjamin too eccentric to be pleasurable. Izzy, by default, became Benjamin's only true companion—as it turned out, a lifelong companion. It also kept Izzy from forming true long-term relationships that might exclude her son. Her husband had died in a vehicle accident when Benjamin was young, for which she was grateful, for he had little tolerance for his son's abstractness. From then on, it was easier for her to abstain from outside relationships for the sake of her son. She understood his peculiarities and found them not that disturbing, perhaps because he was her son. Others, however, did not abide him for long, for he did not comprehend those little niceties that allow people to overlook one's faults.

Izzy, because of a nature which tended to be hard and coarse, worked in an environment that needed that kind of dispassionate discernment. She was no pushover and instinctively knew the games played by the troubled youth in the institutions in which she taught. She maintained tight control over her classrooms and was not easily manipulated by the children for whom destructive manipulation seemed to be natural or was a natural by-product of their dysfunctional home lives.

By Izzy's account, Benjamin's eccentricities were mild and harmless in comparison. He may have been socially inept, but he was not naturally cruel or devious as were many of the children and adults with whom she was used to dealing. And so she saw her son as a delight in an odd way. She enjoyed seeing the naïve manner in which he lived in the world, the wonder that he expressed at unusual events and queer historical artifacts. She had marveled at the fact that he seemed to need nothing but his odd little things and her to be content.

What Izzy did not know is that Benjamin was beginning to see that his mother was growing old and would not be around forever. At his age, he was finally realizing that he was not going to be normal, that he was not going to engage those whom he hoped to impress, even though these occasions were rare. He was stuck in his inability to see what others expected but was coming to understand that. This was the basis for his recent depression, this realization of an inexplicable yet unavoidable future isolation. His mother had always been interested in his activities and notions as few others had. She was irreplaceable.

He had joined clubs at the insistence of his mother when he was younger. These clubs invariably touched on his interests but did not command his interests. At some point, he would deviate from the mission and activities of the club and, in demanding that the club change to suit his developing and diverging interests, would be asked to leave. This was why he ultimately began his antique business in his mother's garage: to solicit the interests of others that might align with his own. Unfortunately, little had happened to accomplish this goal.

"I still say there is no proof that there is a treasure!" Lowler snorted dismissively.

"Of course there is no proof!" Benjamin retorted. "The proof would be in finding the gold, and nobody has found it yet! Did you know that there is an inscription on the gold watch that belonged to James Vanderlin? It is believed that Eli Wilkes had the inscription done before he was murdered!"

Elizabeth and Jason were stunned. "What?" they spoke in stereo.

Benjamin was positively glowing with his achieved effect. "The watch is in a museum in Virginia City. I actually saw it when Mom took me to Virginia City a couple of years ago!"

"Well, what does it say?" Elizabeth and Jason voiced, again in stereo.

"As best I can remember, it says that Vanderlin will never get what he wants until he can admire and appreciate Eli Wilkes! Some people speculate that it is a reference to this painting!"

"What do you mean, Bennie?" Izzy asked.

Benjamin addressed his mother but included all in the room.

"Some scholars think that the message in the watch means that to get what he wanted, in other words his treasure back, Vanderlin would have had to come and look at this painting. The clue is in this painting!"

"That's absurd! Talk about reaching for meanings that are ridiculous!" Lowler sneered.

"Have you seen the watch?" Benjamin challenged Vincent.

"I actually have!" Lowler responded. "I went to Virginia City and to that museum when I was doing research on restoring this place."

"And does it say what Bennie said?" Izzy questioned, clearly defensive of her son.

"Yes," Lowler admitted. "In a paraphrase. But that doesn't mean that is what it means! It is not even certain that it was Eli that had it inscribed! That's just part of the story. It makes a better story, or legend if you will, if it was Eli that did the inscription. There is no proof and the inscription was not signed, so the inscription may have been done by James himself!"

"Yeah right!" Benjamin took his turn expressing disgust. "As if James Vanderlin would inscribe to himself that he must admire Eli Wilkes to get what he wants!"

"The truth is that there is no real way to know who inscribed it or who it was referring to. Eli Wilkes is not even mentioned in the inscription, so we don't know if he was the one to be admired or that it was Vanderlin who needed to do the admiring! All we know is that it was James Vanderlin's watch. We don't know who or what the inscription refers to. For all we know, James Vanderlin may have bought the watch from someone who already had it inscribed!"

These words by Vincent Lowler seemed to put an end to the discussion and, little by little, those in the room filed out to dinner.

CHAPTER 12

California Trail (1850)

James Vanderlin rode a short distance west from where he had deposited William Edwards's body. He stopped his horse to consider where he was. He had ridden for an entire day to the southeast of Humboldt Wells. It was beginning to grow quite dark, and he would have to camp for the night soon. He looked around and found that he was heading into a small valley between two hills. This would be an adequate place to spend the night—no water, but a fire would be shielded by the hills from distant eyes. He hobbled both his and Edwards's horses and began kindling the fire. There was only rabbit grass to use, which would not last long in any event but would be enough to warm the biscuits, bacon, and some coffee. He was glad suddenly that he had kept Edwards's blanket after having rolled Edwards from it down into the gully, for he would need the extra blanket when the chill hit in the middle of the night.

After eating the biscuits and bacon, James sat on his blanket, leaned against his saddle, and watched the fire dwindle into embers. He drank the last of the hot coffee and thought about the road ahead. He was probably closer in distance to the Hastings Cutoff of the California Trail, a cutoff that diverged from the main trail way back near South Pass in the Wyoming Territory and traveled south past the Great Salt Lake. Having traveled southeast from Humboldt Wells for an entire day, James calculated that he was presently somewhere between Big Springs and Mound Springs near the Hastings Cutoff. There would be water there, but he didn't know how far away it was. Perhaps it would be better to go back to Humboldt Wells where the trail was better known to him.

The problem was the other wagons in the group with whom he had traveled. Would they have had time to get to Humboldt Wells? He did not want to reconnect with that group, for there would have been many questions regarding William Edwards. Without his wagon, which he had traded to Jasper Farley for his horse and saddle, he didn't necessarily need to travel with a wagon train. He could follow the California Trail all of the way to California on his own, or he could hook up with others going in the same direction. He could travel much faster on his horse than could the oxen-pulled wagons. But, as he recalled from the wagon train's maps, the Hastings Cutoff headed south from here along and around the Ruby Mountains before it curled back north, meeting up again with the California Trail near the south fork of the Humboldt River Gorge overlook. Those were a lot of extra miles to travel and ultimately might put him back on the California Trail at perhaps the same time as the Farleys and Ben Bennett.

James decided that he would retrace his path back to Humboldt Wells, riding his horse hard to beat the rest of the wagons in the Farley/Bennett group. He felt confident that he could be at Humboldt Wells before those wagons because he now had two horses, which he could switch riding. He lay down and fell immediately into a deep sleep from which he would not rise until the sun was well into the morning sky. The next morning, James rose, packed the horses, watered them from his canteen, and began the journey back to Humboldt Wells. He left without breakfast, wanting to ride right away, and ate hardtack as he rode.

He reached Humboldt Wells that evening just before dark and camped by one of the water holes. No one else was there. He figured he would be able to leave the next morning before the advent of any other known travelers, and that would settle the problem of William Edwards forever. Anyone else he might meet on the trail would have no foreknowledge of the events that had recently occurred. It was possible that the Jasper/Bennett group would wait at Humboldt Wells for the rest of the wagon train that had not been able to afford the ferry crossing of the Snake River. That would put them significantly behind James on the road to California.

For the first time since the deaths of Josie and Jessie, James relaxed. Since their deaths, he had been obsessed with revenge and righteous purpose and had not thought about them in any real context other than as motivation for his intended actions. Suddenly he didn't have that anxious need. He sat next to a real fire of dead wood near water and felt the weight of his situation. With despair, he realized he could not recall their faces in any fixed memory. It had been less than a week, and already, they were fading from his recollection. It was not possible, he thought, and tried to drive the notion of them into his mind. He felt confused, almost nauseous, with the conflicting emotions of loss and self-condemnation. He focused on his watch, a watch that Jessie had given him just weeks before they started on this ill-fated journey, to place their images in his memory.

With the images of Josie and Jessie finally stable in his mind, James fell asleep sitting up against a boulder. He woke when he slumped to the side and bumped his head against a rock. He sat up startled and looked around in the dark. He saw the image of a man barely discernible against the black of the night, slightly illuminated by the diminishing glow from the failing embers of the campfire. The man stood in the darkness, not moving, and appeared to be staring at James. He was slightly back from the ring of light cast off by the embers of the campfire, and it seemed to James that the man had stopped moving suddenly, probably when James tipped over and awakened.

In spite of the suspicious nature of the situation, James was not afraid. His rifle was next to the saddle, which was well within reach, but James made no attempt to get it. He simply sat up and stared back at the man.

Then he said nonchalantly, "You might as well come into the light and sit down. I can make some more coffee if you want it."

The man did as he was bidden. He was not a tall man, perhaps six inches shorter than James, but he was thick. He was older and had a curled gray beard, which was unkempt. His hat was well used and floppy, loose around the brim that covered the nature in his eyes. His clothes were dusty but still serviceable, and his coat was long and rimmed in fur. He carried a long cap-and-ball musket in his right hand, and a large wood-handled knife protruded from a thick leather belt at his waist. The man plopped down, crossing his legs, across from James on the other side of the embers. James reached over and stoked the embers with a stick, bringing up the flames. He threw more wood on the fire and braced the coffeepot atop the flames. Neither man said anything until the pot could be heard boiling, at which time James procured a metal cup from his saddlebag and poured coffee for the man.

The stranger took the cup from James and nodded his thanks. His face was tanned and lined above the beard. It was difficult to judge his age because of his worn and weathered visage, but he was certainly older than James. He did not seem to present any danger but appeared content to silently sip his coffee. Neither man spoke for many minutes; They did not attempt to look at each other but stared into the fire, seemingly lost in thought or reflection.

Finally, the man spoke.

"Sun'll be up soon," he declared. "Name's Jed Belleau. Head'n west or east?" he asked without looking up.

"West," James answered.

"Mind if I tag along for a way?" Jed continued. "Better to have company through this part of the country. Shoshone are kicking up a storm hereabouts. Killed some pilgrims not far from here. Massacred the lot—took their hair, horses, butchered the oxen. I would'a buried 'em, but didn't want to stick around too long."

James's ears perked up.

"Do you know who they were?" James asked intently. "Their names—anything?"

"Don' know. Four wagons, burned up. Seven or eight dead. Three or four men, a couple women, a couple kids. The savages must have taken everything they could carry and burned the rest. Nothin' left."

James exhaled and leaned back against the boulder. He had been holding his breath and hadn't realized it. Jed Belleau looked at him stealthily from below the brim of his hat.

"You know 'em?" he asked.

James collected himself, paused, and answered slowly.

"Maybe. I traveled with a bunch like that for a time. I went on ahead to look for game and water. I have been sticking around the Wells, keeping close to water, looking for game."

Jed Belleau glanced around.

"No luck with the game?" Jed asked.

"Not much," James replied sullenly, shutting down the conversation. He realized the topic was entering dangerous territory and didn't want this stranger delving too deeply into his circumstances. Jed Belleau shrugged and went back to drinking his coffee as if he understood that the topic of conversation had come to a close. After a time, he stood up and tossed the empty cup toward James's pack.

"Got to go get my rig," he declared and strode off into the darkness. He came back minutes later pulling three mules that were laden with supplies. He hobbled the mules next to James's horses and came back to the fire.

"Figured I'd get a couple hours of sleep before we move on," Jed said as he lay down on a blanket and shortly began snoring.

James sat for a time and studied the sleeping figure. He was unsure what to make of Jed Belleau. This was not a simple traveler like those James was used to. More likely, Jed was a mountain man or trapper. James knew that the Hudson Bay Company paid trappers in this part of the country for pelts, but James could not discern any significant amount of furs on the pack animals standing partly in the light cast off by the campfire. Perhaps Jed Belleau carried supplies to miners or prospectors, for his mules seemed more equipped for that kind of enterprise. Parts of the mule packs were covered by tarps of canvas so it was difficult to distinguish their contents, but the shapes underneath were certainly not consistent to the fur trade. More like boxes. Or perhaps Jed was a prospector himself, and the supplies were to keep him in the desolate wilderness for a time.

James shortly gave up his speculations and again drifted off to sleep sitting up against the boulder. He had pulled a blanket over him before falling asleep and was grateful in the morning when the sun began breaching his eyelids and he found a layer of frost coating the blanket. Jed Belleau already had coffee cooking on a rekindled fire and was greasing a pan to fry a potato with bacon.

"Gonna be a beautiful day," Jed said, sitting on his haunches while placing the pan over the fire. "Good day to travel."

And so it was. After putting everything in order on their animals, the two men started west following the Humboldt River.

CHAPTER 13

The Bed-and-Breakfast on Silver Street

Andy Walch was sitting in the breakfast room across the table from Benjamin Dulles, eating a donut with both hands. It was unclear whether he was listening to Benjamin because his concentration seemed totally on the donut.

"I can't believe you have never heard of Virginia City!" Benjamin was exclaiming with animation. "Have you never even watched *Bonanza?*"

Andy looked sideways at Benjamin, stuffing his mouth with the donut. He didn't answer but Benjamin continued anyway.

"Virginia City is one of the most famous cities in the United States! It was the place of one of the biggest gold and silver discoveries in the history of the world! Mark Twain worked there before he was Mark Twain, before he had written any of his great books!"

Andy shrugged and continued stuffing the donut into his mouth. There were three more sitting on the plate in front of him. He was not a tall man and was certainly not a small man. He was rotund, a natural consequence of his passion for pastries. He did not care at all about what Benjamin Dulles was yammering on about, but he was thinking about lunch.

"Why did you come here?" Benjamin challenged, undaunted in his need to confront Andy's indifference.

"Ed wanted to," Andy mumbled through his chewing. "I wasn't doing anything anyway, so I came with."

"Ed wanted to do what?" The voice belonged to Ed Walch who had just entered the room.

"Your cousin doesn't know anything about Virginia City or James Vanderlin or anything!" Benjamin ejaculated, shaking his head.

Ed Walch laughed. "I think you already know what Andy's passion is, and it is not history. I'm the history buff in our family. Andy was the only one that I could talk into coming along." Ed's laugh turned to a smile. "He's good that way." He was affectionately watching his cousin devour the last donut.

"I was trying to explain to your cousin why I thought the painting in the drawing room contained clues to the location of James Vanderlin's gold!" Benjamin recounted with exasperation.

"I would be interested in that," Ed responded sincerely.

"Finally, someone who will listen!" Benjamin had almost given up on communicating with those around him, having failed to elicit any positive responses to his theories. He had a lifetime of people thinking he was an eccentric crackpot, but he had never been able to acknowledge it. He would always believe he was right in whatever he thought and couldn't understand why others were not immediately taken with his notions. In the end, he simply dismissed them as being intellectually inferior.

"What clues are contained in the painting in the salon?" Ed encouraged.

Just then, Vincent Lowler stepped into the room. He was carrying dishes to set the table for lunch and plopped them down onto the table with a porcelan clunk.

"Am I interrupting something?" he asked politely.

"Benjamin was about to explain what clues to the location of James Vanderlin's gold were in the painting in the other room," Ed explained.

"Oh forget it!" Benjamin huffed and stormed out of the room.

Ed and Vincent looked at each other in surprise.

"What got into him?" Vincent asked as he began placing the china about the table, trying to avoid moving Andy from in front of his empty donut plate.

"I have no idea," Ed responded. "Maybe he thought we were making fun of him." He shrugged as he said this and sat next to Andy. "What do think about this gold business?" He addressed the question to Vincent.

Vincent stopped his table setting for a moment to consider the question.

"I wish it were true," he said. "But then again, if someone ever finds the gold, the allure of getting people to come here to look for the gold would end. I would probably go bankrupt and have to close the place."

People started to file in for lunch. First Izzy came with Elizabeth, whom she had run into on the stairs. Jason sidled up behind them and poked his sister in the ribs playfully. Marjorie and Marvin Cosgrove entered the room hand in hand. Izzy and Elizabeth smiled at each other and commented quietly how sweet it was to see a couple still in love after twenty some years of marriage. The Cosgroves seemed truly a partnership, rarely appearing anywhere apart. They finished each other's statements unembarrassed, appearing not even to notice. Elizabeth wondered aloud, but quietly, to Izzy and Jason whether Marjorie and Marvin had ever had a fight. Elizabeth made a mental note to ask them this very question when she had the chance, for it was the kind of thing that fascinated her. She actually believed that it was possible for two people to be so compatible that overt fighting never occurred. Jason and Izzy, on the other hand, had no such beliefs and scoffed when Elizabeth suggested it.

Lunch occurred in a friendly, supportive tone of conversation on the parts of everyone present. Not present was Benjamin Dulles. Izzy became concerned and, at one point, excused herself to go look for him. She returned in a very few minutes and, upon questioning by Vincent Lowler, informed that Benjamin was in the next room, the salon, studying the painting of Eli Wilkes. Izzy shook her head and wondered aloud about Benjamin's intense fascination with the picture.

"I believe he thinks he has solved the puzzle over James Vanderlin's gold," declared Ed Walch.

"Is that so?" several people voiced simultaneously, all suddenly interested in the one conversation.

"He believes the painting shows the location," Ed continued.

This began a hubbub of conversation around the topic of James Vanderlin and Eli Wilkes. Many views regarding the actuality of there being a treasure were discussed as well as the proposed natures of both James Vanderlin and Eli Wilkes. For the most part, Eli was considered the unfortunate victim and James the evil villain in everyone's view. In a very short time, Benjamin Dulles and his fascination with the painting were forgotten, and the lunch was completed. People drifted out of the dining room and went about their separate ways. Elizabeth, Jason, and Ed Walch walked together to the Stockmen's Hotel nearby on Commercial Street to do a little gambling at the slot machines. Izzy wanted to go to a bookstore on Idaho Street but could find no one to go with her. Since she could not find Benjamin, who had left the salon and did not answer her knock on his door, she went by herself. The Cosgroves went back to their room to take a nap, and Andy Walch walked down to the bowling alley on River Street. Vincent Lowler cleaned up the dining room and began preparations for dinner.

Jason Ryder played Twenty-One at a table in the Stockmen's after losing forty dollars on slots. He hoped to win the money back at the table but lost twenty-five more. Elizabeth seemed to be keeping her own on the slot machines, at one time being ahead one hundred and thirty dollars, but then lost all but twenty of the additional dollars in the end. They lost track of Ed Walch after the first hour and didn't see him again until dinner. Dinner was at six o'clock and everyone appeared except for, once again, Benjamin Dulles. By this time, Izzy was exasperated with her son's moods and muttered the same to Elizabeth, next to whom she sat.

"I'm gonna go get him!" she declared and left the table.

Marjorie Cosgrove realized that she had forgotten her purse in her room and went upstairs to get it. She passed by Benjamin Dulles's room, from which the door was partially open, and heard agonizing sobs coming from the room. Curious and somewhat alarmed, she opened the door wider to ask if she could help with whatever was going on and saw Izzy leaning over Benjamin, cradling him in her arms, rocking him while she moaned in pain.

"Izzy?" Marjorie uttered, stepping into the room.

Izzy turned her head to Marjorie and began wailing. Marjorie was stunned. Benjamin was lying in Izzy's arms turned partially on his back with a large kitchen knife sticking out from his chest. Blood had soaked his blue shirt and the beige-and-orange bedspread on the bed and had covered the front of Izzy's gray suit.

"Oh my god!" Marjorie screamed, standing in the door, unable to move. The wailing of Izzy and the scream of Marjorie startled everyone in the dining room downstairs, and all but Andy made a mad dash for the stairs to see what was the matter. Marvin Cosgrove was the first to reach the second floor landing, having realized instantly his wife's desperate scream. He moved her aside to enter the room of Benjamin Dulles. It took him but seconds to assess the situation and to take command of those filing up the stairs.

"Tell Vincent to call the police!" he yelled down the stairs to all those within earshot. "Ben's been stabbed!"

Jason immediately left the stairs and hurried down to the basement to alert Vincent Lowler who was in the process of ascending the stairs. He had heard the general cry of alarm and had begun to climb to the ground floor when Jason intercepted him. He quickly descended for the telephone. After phoning the police, Vincent hurried to the second floor to view the catastrophe. Everyone was milling about outside Benjamin's room, not knowing what to do but not willing to leave. No one spoke—it was as if everyone was holding their breath, waiting for the moment to retreat back in time, hoping that it was all a mistake.

"Is he dead?" someone, a soft male voice, finally whispered.

"I think so!" came a whisper back, this time female. "Did you see? There is a knife in his chest!"

"I don't believe it!" another female whispered. "This is crazy! It can't be true!"

"Believe it!" proclaimed Marvin Cosgrove in a harsh whisper. "I saw it! He's dead all right!"

CHAPTER 14

The Wall Defile (1850)

                    Jed Belleau returned to the campsite from the river, which was but fifty feet away. He and James Vanderlin had ridden leisurely to get to the Wall Defile, also known as the Fremont Canyon for explorer John Fremont who had sent a party down this part of the Humboldt River in 1845 and is the site of present-day Carlin Canyon. It took several days for the two of them to make this journey, with Jed's mules so laden down that they had to walk leading the animals the entire way. James was unconcerned now that they would be overtaken by Ben Bennett's party. He knew that, even with Jasper Farley driving James's wagon—which was far better and faster moving than Jasper's old farm wagon—the party would not move as fast as James and Jed were traveling.

    The singing of the birds echoing off the vertical walls of the canyon was somehow inspiring to James. For the first time since his loss, he felt a small, tiny sense of a world apart from his pain. He was no longer nervous about what he had done to

William Edwards, confident that he would not be found out. It was not remorse that he had been feeling but a notion of fleeing from some desperate urgency. He had needed to move or escape, or he believed that he would perish. It was not a rational conviction, more of a suspicion or superstition. And yet James was not a superstitious person. He trusted only himself and his self-will. There had never been a doubt in James's mind that he could do whatever was necessary, and he had done what he believed was necessary: necessary to his need for completion and revenge.

This is what brought him to this place—this canyon in the middle of a desolate wilderness, this piece of marvelous nature dug into the merciless mountains. In 1841, the Bidwell-Bartleson party became the first emigrant group to thread its way through Wall Defile. Two years later, the Walker-Chiles party—traversing the California Trail from Fort Hall, Idaho—rolled the first wagons through. Over the next decades, hundreds of thousands of men, women, and children bound for California passed this way. It was a canyon cut by the Humboldt River through one of the many north/south mountain ranges that litter the west.

The Humboldt River was the last discovered of the American rivers. It was first named by Peter Skene Ogden, a trapper and explorer. It was called Mary's River after Ogden's Indian wife, then the Barren River for its lack of trees, and finally placed on maps as the Humboldt River, named after the German naturalist Alexander von Humboldt. The Humboldt River traces an east-west arc through Nevada's northern desert, and its river plain was the route for the emigrants heading to the California gold fields. Its waters were alkaline, brackish, and sometimes nonexistent but sustained grasses that allowed traveler's animals to survive the journey through Nevada's harsh desert. This was the path that would lead James Vanderlin to California.

Perhaps it was the birds that spooked Jed Belleau's mules. A tremendous shriek was heard reverberating off the walls of the canyon and then the thunder of hundreds of wings as a cloud of birds spiraled through the canyon overhead. The mules bolted as a group, followed by James's horses. They broke the hobbles that had kept them stationary and raced up the canyon back the way they had come. The horses stopped almost immediately due to the fact that they were tied together and one of the hobbles held. The mules ran up the canyon, gaining speed as various items fell from their packs, lightening their loads. Jed Belleau stood for a moment, flabbergasted, and then ran after them screaming at the top of his lungs.

James corralled his horses, moved them back to the campsite, and untied the unhobbled horse from its restrained partner. He secured the still-hobbled horse to a cylindrical rock, mounted the unfettered horse barebacked, and raced after Jed Belleau and the mules. Passing Jed at a gallop, he shouted for him to go back to camp; he would catch the mules. Jed stopped running, bent over and laboriously trying to catch his breath. He began collecting items strewn about the riverbed and resolutely walked back to the campsite. The mules had stopped in a group around the bend of river and beyond the sight of the campsite. They were no longer afraid and leisurely drank from the river at their feet.

James drew each mule from the shallow edge of the river and began resecuring the packs. It was then that he noticed the quantity of women's hair tied to a string and secured under one of the loose tarps. It was not just the women's hair; there were several men's ears that had been cut from Caucasian heads, pierced and tied together in a garish necklace that had been secured to the strand of women's hair. James was instantly taken aback, not appalled for he had heard of men of the wilderness taking scalps from natives that they had killed. But these were not native scalps or ears. Some of the hair was blond, some brunette. None were the coarse black hair of the native tribes.

James began searching the packs under the loose tarps. He found numerous items of jewelry and personal gold such as watches and cufflinks and tie pins. A watch was inscribed: "To my Randall, from your Elisabeth, with all my love." A chill passed over James. Randall Whitehouse's wife was named Elisabeth! Elisabeth had died along with his Josie and Jessie. James searched further until he found the quilt that Ben Bennett's wife had made and proudly displayed to Josie in front of James. It was a beautifully embroidered and hand-sewn bedspread of blue and gold that represented their future in California. James stopped searching and stood leaning against the mule, his face covered in sweat.

The picture took on clarity in James's mind. Jed Belleau said that he had come upon a set of wagons that had been ravaged by savages. But savages would have taken at least some of these items, especially the bedspread and the trinkets. As James looked around at the items littering the ground in front of him and those things still on the mules, he realized that they were pillaged items. They didn't follow any pattern of use for a lone traveler other than as saleable or tradeable goods. James formed a picture in his mind of Jed Belleau riding into the Bennett camp claiming to be a proficient guide and weary traveler. He saw Jed take his time to assess their strength and their trust and then massacre them one by one, probably at night and in their sleep. He would then have all of the time in the world to go through their things to pick what he wanted before setting the camp to torch.

James began looking at the mules more closely and believed at least one of them might have belonged to Jasper Farley. This presented a real dilemma to James. It wasn't that he mourned the deaths of the others; he didn't feel one way or another for them. But now Jed Belleau must assume what had just happened. He must believe that James had seen the evidence of his crimes and must do something about that. James considered his plight. He had jumped aboard his horse barebacked. His rifle lay next to his saddle at the campsite, and he had no pistol. All he had was the folding knife that was always in his pocket.

He renewed his search of the pack animals. He found three rifles of various calibers secured to the base of one of the packs, one of which had W. Bradley carved into the stock. James had seen this very rifle not more than ten days ago when Willard Bradley had shot a gopher from his wagon and then bragged about how good gopher meat had been. James put that information aside and continued searching but found no ammunition. There were no pistols or knives or anything that could be used effectively as weapons. He stopped to think. It was possible that Jed Belleau would not shoot James as James walked back into camp. It was possible that he would wait to find how much James actually knew. Additionally, shooting James as he came back into camp might once again spook the animals, and that would not be smart. He would then have to find his mules, the horse, and his ill-gotten goods all over again.

It would be smarter for Jed to try to allay James's fears, explain away his possessions in some believable story and then kill James in his sleep, as he had likely done the wagon party. This was the more probable scenario, and James felt fairly certain that Jed would stick to a method that had worked well in the past. James was not unfamiliar to the mental workings of those around him, having had much experience as a corrupt constable for many years. He was used to figuring out motivations toward maximizing his ability to manipulate individuals for his own gain.

With that in mind, James began collecting and securing the fallen items back onto the packs and made his way back to the campsite. He rounded the corner of the cliff gingerly, hoping that his expectations of Jed were true, half expecting to hear the sound of a gunshot and feeling the impact of a projectile. Nothing! Jed Belleau was kneeling next to the fire facing James and casually pouring coffee from the pot into a cup. He sipped the coffee as if no concern entered his mind. He did keep James in his stare from below the brim of his hat, his eyes never leaving James as James approached. James smiled in his mind; Jed was doing exactly as he thought he would. He was studying James, trying to calculate how much time he had before he would have to kill James, wanting to delay the event to a more calculated time. Jed was casual, presenting the appearance of unconcern, but James knew that in Jed's mind he was preparing to do the evil deed.

"Well that wasn't so bad," James commented affably, comfortably, trying to make Jed feel at ease. "The mules didn't go far beyond the bend. Not much was lost from the packs, not much to put back. How'd it go here?"

Jed seemed to relax somewhat. His plan would work now. He had planned to kill James Vanderlin anyway, to take his horses, but he wanted a better place. He was waiting for a place where the event would be easy to conceal and the circumstances would be more suited to his purpose. Since they had been together, Vanderlin had been too alert for Jed to be able to complete what Jed intended, in the way that he intended. Perhaps it was what he had said about the wagon group that made Vanderlin wary. It didn't matter. Vanderlin would die at his hands, for he couldn't afford to let him live. Besides wanting Vanderlin's horses, Vanderlin had known the people from the wagon group, and that left Jed in a precarious dilemma. Vanderlin may or may not have seen anything on Jed's pack mules, but sooner or later, Vanderlin would figure out what happened. He would see something in Jed's stuff that would make sense of it all, and that would be it for Jed.

"No problem," Jed said casually. "Here, let me do that!" James had begun tightening the canvas tarp over the back of a mule, and Jed stood up and went to complete the task. He didn't want to take any chance on Vanderlin seeing something at this late juncture while he was messing with the tarp. Jed took the cord from James's hand and pulled tight to tie it to the pack frame. He felt a sharp pain in his side and took a step back, raised his arm, and looked at the folding knife protruding from between his ribs. Shock took over his features as he looked up at James Vanderlin whose hand still clasped the knife. James withdrew the knife and stabbed Jed Belleau again and then again.

Jed Belleau collapsed to his knees beside the mule. His mind could not fully grasp what had just happened. His eyes never left the face of James Vanderlin as he sat feeling his lungs fill up with blood. Vanderlin's face remained calm, like a mask. Jed waited in confusion for some sign to flash across Vanderlin's face that would explain, but nothing happened. James Vanderlin did not waiver in watching Jed die. He simply stood there and watched—not angry, not gleeful, not anything. He was totally devoid of emotion. It was as if Vanderlin was watching a sunset or a cloud cover the moon. There was no attachment at all to what was happening. At least Jed enjoyed the feeling he got when he killed, he thought mournfully as he died.

James watched Jed Belleau slip prone to the soft sand and watched the death rattle of his final moments. When he was certain that Belleau was dead, he went back to the fire and poured a cup of coffee, which he leisurely drank.

CHAPTER 15

Marshall Dillon

Frank Dillon had been a homicide detective with the Elko Police Department for seven years and had been a cop in Elko for eleven years. He had come to Elko in retirement from the Los Angeles County Sheriff's Department where he had over twenty-five years' experience—fifteen of those years working in homicide. He had seen many bodies in his career, and this one was not unique. Benjamin Dulles's room at the bed-and-breakfast on Silver Street had been cordoned off, and Frank was standing still at the door, surveying the room with his eyes.

Frank was fifty-nine years old and looked it. He had left Los Angeles to get away from that earth scorched with corruption and to think about something other than dead bodies and interoffice political intrigue. He came to Elko jaded, wanting to renew himself as something else. It didn't work. After two years of sitting at home, a newly built and purchased home in Spring Creek, and trying various work-at-home enterprises, he broke down and admitted he was going crazy with boredom.

His wife of nine years, the third Mrs. Dillon, demanded that he go get a job and stick with it, or she would leave him.

It turned out police work was all Frank was good at. Once he accepted this, it wasn't so bad. He did renew himself within the police culture and began enjoying the job again. There weren't that many homicides in Elko, so Frank was able to attend to other facets of police work. He started a civilian ride-along program that was growing in stature. He had just begun teaching a class at the community college in community policing and was actually enjoying the wonder and vitality of his students. He felt his accumulated cynicism start to slip away and wondered why he hadn't tried this years ago.

"Who found the body?" Frank asked the first responder, Officer Michelle Neubrander.

"The mother," Michelle responded. "She is downstairs in the dining room."

Frank continued to look about the room without moving from the spot near the doorway.

"Was he moved at all?" he asked.

"From what I understand, the mother held him for some time after she found him. I believe she sat on the bed holding him on her lap. At least, that is what the witnesses say. She wouldn't let go until the EMTs made her move downstairs."

"How many witnesses?" Frank inquired.

"Six," Michelle said. "I have all their names. They are all staying here. There is a seventh guy staying here, but he never came up to the room. And there is a cook, a housekeeper, and a dishwasher. They were here when the body was discovered, but they don't stay here. They're locals."

"All right," Frank murmured. Then more pronounced, he said, "Let's get the room swept by forensics, then let's button it down. No one comes in here till we are completely done with this thing. I want it taped off. No one who was staying here leaves for now."

Frank turned and gestured to the forensic crew standing in the hall outside the room. All wore white coveralls with the emblem of the Elko Police Department emblazoned on the breast and across the back and hair caps and foot booties of cloth. Among them were members of the coronor's office, awaiting their turn to examine and remove the body. Frank descended the stairs to the dining room where Izzy sat with her head down on the table, her hands clasped together across her lap. She looked up when Frank addressed her. Her eyes were red and swollen, and her expression was pained.

"I'm so sorry for your loss," Frank began gently, sincerely, touching her shoulder lightly. He sat down next to her and leaned toward her. "If there is anything I can do to help you, I will."

Izzy's expression changed suddenly. Her eyes narrowed, her brows furrowed, and she scowled.

"Just catch the son of a bitch who did this!" she spat out vehemently. Then, just as quickly, her visage went back to the pained expression of moments ago. She began quietly sobbing, her head bowed.

"We will, ma'am," Frank reassured her. "Can you tell me anything about what happened before finding your son? Was anyone angry at him, or did anyone have a grudge against him?"

"No-o-o!" she cried plaintively. "No one! That's just it! No one disliked my Bennie! He never hurt anyone! He was just Bennie—my Bennie! He never hurt anyone!"

"Okay" Frank said, trying to be comforting but needing to press for information. "How did you happen to find him?"

Izzy struggled to recall. "He missed two meals. It was not like him. At dinner, I went to find him. I knocked on his door, but he didn't answer. I opened the door to see if he had taken anything like a jacket or his book bag to tell me where he had gone, and I saw him lying across the bed with a knife sticking out of his chest!" She gasped again in a sob.

"When you came up to look for him, did you notice anything or anyone out of place? Something unusual or something that didn't seem right?" Frank asked.

"No. Just that he had missed two meals. That was unusual."

"When did you last see him alive?"

"He didn't come in for lunch, so I went to find him. I thought maybe he just forgot, lost track of time. He was in the drawing room looking at that painting. When I asked what he was doing, he muttered something about finding something that had been missing. But he wouldn't leave the painting. I figured it was one of his little obsessions, so I left him and went back to finish lunch."

"What happened then?"

"I don't know. Lunch finished and everyone went their separate ways. I wanted to go to a bookstore and went to find out if Bennie wanted to go with, but then I couldn't find him."

"What do you mean you couldn't find him?"

"He wasn't in the drawing room anymore. And I knocked on his door but he didn't answer, so I assumed he had gone somewhere. I went to the bookstore by myself."

"Did you run into anyone else while you were out?"

"No. I didn't see anyone else until I got back and came down for dinner."

"Thank you, Izzy," Frank said, standing up from the table. "Again, if I can do anything to help you, please let me know."

Frank Dillon left Izzy in the dining room, followed by Michelle Neubrander. He walked into the drawing room to look at the painting.

"You know, I heard about this painting when I first got to Elko," he commented pensively. "What do you know about it?"

Michelle thought awhile.

"Not much really. I understand it was painted by a local artist back in 1872. It was supposedly commissioned by Eli Wilkes, the guy in the painting. No one knows why, in truth, although there is a lot of speculation. Wilkes was shot in this very room not long after the painting was hung there, and it has hung there ever since. I guess it's kind of famous."

"I heard it was supposed to be the way to find some kind of treasure," Frank mentioned.

Michelle smiled. "That's the story," she answered.

Michelle Neubrander was tiny. She looked even smaller in her police department uniform, which was tailored and light blue, and with her dark hair pulled back into a tight bun. By her complexion, she could be Middle Eastern or Hispanic, although she wasn't. She was Norwegian on her mother's side and a mutt on her father's. She did know some high school Spanish but was not very fluent. In Elko there was a small Hispanic community on the south side of the Humboldt River and the railroad tracks, primarily made up of hotel workers. She tried out her Spanish whenever she was called to that side of town for some type of disturbance, but it wasn't frequent enough for her to truly practice her limited language skills.

Michelle had been a police officer with the Elko Police Department for four years, joining them right out of college. She had majored in Criminal Justice at UNR in Reno but wanted to return to Elko where she had grown up, to the delight of her parents and numerous aunts, uncles, and cousins. She was a boon to the police department, for with just her relatives, not including her many friends, she had the makings of a first-rate intelligence operation. For anything that needed to be known about Elko County, Michelle had a contact of some sort. And while her sexual leanings tended toward women, she was cute enough to almost always curry the interest of men. Michelle was acutely aware of this desire on the part of men and was not opposed to relying on it to achieve a desired result.

Frank looked quizzically at Michelle. "What kind of treasure?" he asked.

"Gold of some sort—coins, jewelry. No one knows for sure. Most people around here consider it a fairy tail, something invented by the owners of the establishment to promote business." Michelle glanced around the well-apportioned room. "Obviously, it's working."

"All right," Frank declared, changing his tone, "let's set up this room as an interview room. Let's get a couple of usable tables and chairs in here and move some of this furniture back against the walls." Then, as if realizing that he had overstepped his boundaries, he squared off in front of Michelle. "What are you doing now? I mean, would you feel comfortable helping me with this investigation?"

Michelle responded with enthusiasm, "Absolutely! If you can square it with my sergeant, I would love to help!"

"Consider it done," Frank said with certainty, as indeed it was. A case of this magnitude would allow Frank many privileges when it came to funding the investigation. Drug deals gone wrong or domestic homicides were the typical homicide in most venues, and Frank would have handled them in a standard way. But this was different. This was a high-profile murder, one in which a tourist was murdered by someone unknown and with unknown motives, potentially causing much fear in the community. It had to be investigated expeditiously and thoroughly. That would involve more than the normal expense and more than the normal personnel. As there were only two detectives qualified to conduct homicide investigations at the police department—and since James Erickson, the other homicide detective, was on vacation—Frank would be able to tap other officers for assistance.

Frank was familiar with Michelle Neubrander. He was aware of her background and connections in the Elko area as well as the rumors about her personal life. Frank cared a lot about the connections and little about the rumors. Coming from Los Angeles, he was of the opinion that a person's off-duty activities, as long as they were not illegal or unethical, should remain the business of that person. He was of an age where he appreciated Michelle's obvious enthusiasm and bountiful energy and was immune to the fact that she was a doll. As opposed to many of the men that he worked with, he did not see himself as the answer to every woman's suspected loneliness and need for physical fulfillment. He saw himself as a slightly overweight, beginning-to-bald, late middle-aged man who was lucky to have found his wife when he did. He believed that his wife only loved him now because her love for him began when he was still somewhat attractive. She loved him before he had degenerated into the old man that he felt like nowadays.

"I need to tell you upfront that this is not going to be a simple thing for you," Frank admonished sternly in a fatherly manner. "This will not be like regular work. There are no set hours. We sleep when we can, and sometimes not enough. We go where the leads take us and when they take us. You will be doing a lot of running around for me, a lot of legwork—"

"I'm fine with that," Michelle interrupted.

Frank held up his hand. "Hear it all before you sign on. I will try to explain what I want and why I want it when I can. Sometimes I might ask you to do something in front of someone and won't explain why. I need you to just do it. You must be willing to do whatever whenever and trust that you will understand why when I get to it. Do you agree to this?"

"Yes," Michelle stated emphatically but less impatiently. She was beginning to hear in Frank's voice the reality of what she would be expected to do. Implied, without actually saying it, was the fact that she would have to drop everything at his whim to do his bidding. This was something that should bother her, this being in the thrall of a man; but strangely, it didn't. She knew Frank Dillon by reputation as a no-nonsense detective who didn't play the typical office games, either political or sexual. She trusted him.

She imagined herself trying to explain this to her recent romantic interest, a woman several years older whom she had met in a grocery store. The nice thing about being in patrol was that once her shift was over, with some exceptions, she was done with the job and could just be herself. She, they, could plan around her schedule. What Frank was saying was that her job would never be done until the investigation was complete and someone was arrested for this heinous crime.

She might have to leave Margo, or whoever, in the middle of whatever to go back on the job. She couldn't drink to impairment, which really meant she couldn't drink at all, or leave town for that occasional hormonal weekend at the spa without Frank's approval.

Michelle considered these things in a second as she answered Frank in the affirmative. While the idea of giving up her life to the job was abhorrent to her, she was sufficiently ambitious to know that working with Frank Dillon on this homicide would go a long way toward cementing her desire to become a detective. She thought of herself as that proverbial sponge willing to soak up whatever Frank Dillon had to offer by way of knowledge. And there was no doubt in anyone's mind that Frank Dillon was knowledgeable about homicides.

"Good!" Frank exclaimed. "Now that that is out of the way, who would you suggest we interview first?"

The first test, Michelle thought, and she answered definitely, "Ed Walch!"

Frank looked surprised. "Why Ed Walch?"

"Because he made a comment about you being 'Marshall Dillon' when you first got here," Michelle responded, appearing serious. Startled, Frank looked at her for a moment and then burst out laughing. It became instantly clear to him that he made the right choice in who to work with and that this woman would bring a sense of humor to the task—something that would become essential as time wore on.

CHAPTER 16

Carson Pass (1850)

James Vanderlin had reached the pinnacle at Kit Carson Pass before his descent into the California gold fields. It had not been an easy journey, and truthfully, he did not know what he would do once he reached Sutter's Fort near where the gold was alleged to have been found two years previous. When he had presented the plan to Josie and Jessie an eternity ago back in Peoria, Illinois, it was without an end. He believed that once he reached California, the path to their happiness and success would become clear to him. Now that he was so close, he had no clue what that path was to be. Not that it mattered anymore. His motivation for riches had been provided by his wife and child and by an inner belief that he could do anything with their happiness in front of him.

He had made the journey to this point, after the deaths of Josie and Jessie, driven by his need to move and with nowhere else to go. California was the destination seared into his mind from months of travel and preparation. It was not really connected now, except as a place to end. It felt to James that he had to get there for Josie and Jessie, to fulfill his promise to them. After that, it didn't matter. He would live or die, for all he cared.

After killing Jed Belleau in the Wall Defile/Fremont Canyon, James had transported the body through the canyon and buried it in the hills outside present-day Carlin. James now had two horses and three mules, with the mules laden down in tradable goods. He unloaded the goods from the mules to decide what he would keep for the journey west. Some of the goods could only bring disaster if their history was discovered, and James had no desire for that outcome. He buried the identifiable goods, including Willard Bradley's rifle and Randall Whitehouse's watch, with Jed Belleau, reasoning that if the body was discovered, the items would become entangled with Belleau and have no connection to James. He had wrapped Belleau's body in the Bennett's quilt for the same reason. During the time that he traveled with Jed, they had met no one on the trail who could associate James to Jed Belleau. James felt reasonably disassociated from Jed Belleau.

The journey from Wall Defile to Gravely Ford went without drama. James crossed the Humboldt River at Gravely Ford to the south side of the river and traveled the south side past Iron Point near present-day Winnemucca, then down to the Humboldt Sink near present-day Lovelock. Between Gravely Ford and Iron Point, following the Humboldt River, James was shadowed by a band of Piute Indians who stayed on the north side of the river. The band, composed of five riders, made James nervous, but they seemed disinterested in James and were not wearing war paint. James assumed that they were a hunting party but wondered if they would see his horses and mules as worthy prizes. He kept a sharp eye on them for approximately twenty miles until they veered north and were lost in the hills.

All of the way to the Humboldt Sink, where the Humboldt River went underground and the Forty-Mile Desert began, James simply followed the river. He met no other travelers and lived on the supplies provided by Jed Belleau and his mules. Near the river there was grass and water for the animals, but James camped at night away from the water and kept campfires to a minimum just in case another Jed Belleau happened by. He had hoped to catch up to a wagon train, to travel with others, but found none on the trail. It was a long, lonely ride that gave James time to ponder. He tried to not think of his loss and, instead, constantly went over the mental map he had devised in his mind from his recollection of the actual item. James was not an explorer or mountain man and had no desire to veer from the well-traveled path. He liked being close to civilization, and regardless of what he thought of other men, he needed their proximity.

The Forty-Mile Desert was a desolate stretch of waterless, alkali wasteland. The first wagon train to come this way was the Walker-Chiles party in 1843, and it was the most dreaded section of the California Trail. Most people tried to travel at night in the summer because of the unbearable heat during the day. This was certainly the case for James, who learned quickly that he and the animals were using too much water trying to cross the desert during the day. He began looking for those rare spots of shade in the morning in the middle of nothing but low scrub brush or chalky white flats, hoping to snatch bits of sleep during the hottest parts of the day. As dusk approached, he would rouse the animals, saddle his horse, and begin the trek into nightfall. This was not a bad way to travel since the landscape was primarily flat with occasional sand dunes, and there were rarely any gaps in the terrain. Still, he had to take it slow in order to keep the animals from stepping into a hole or falling into a waterless wash in the darkness.

James knew he had to conserve water after he had filled up the four water containers in the last vestiges of the Humboldt River before it disappeared into the Humboldt Sink. The Forty-Mile Desert was so named because it was approximately forty miles of desolate wasteland devoid of water before James would be able to replenish his canteens again in the Carson River. The Carson River—named after Kit Carson, an explorer of the area in the 1840s in conjunction with Lieutenant John C. Fremont, then of the US Army Topographical Engineers—flowed in the opposite direction from the Humboldt River. It began in the snowy layers of the Sierra Nevada Mountains and flowed east to the Carson Sink near present-day Fallon. The Humboldt and Carson Rivers were separated by that hated and feared Forty-Mile Desert.

The one consolation of traveling through the Forty-Mile Desert was that James didn't have to fear the presence of renegade Indians. Not even they journeyed through that part of the Utah Territory unless absolutely necessary. More often than not, travelers in that vicinity, to include friendly Indians, would band together to make the trip possible. A lone traveler who became incapacitated through injury or who had succumbed to the elements was likely to die. In a group, there was the potential for survival even if injured. James's concentration then was centered on keeping himself and his animals from dehydration and injury. Traveling at night answered one dilemma but enhanced the other.

At the end of the third night of travel through the desolate expanse, the animals sensed the nearness of water and began acting in a raucous manner. They snorted and pawed the earth, trying to break their bonds to run recklessly toward the perceived moisture. James had to strain to keep them from bolting and was brutal with a stick that he had cut from a mesquite bush for just such a purpose. James made camp and fed the horses and mules the remaining water from his last canteen to keep them calm. He did not want to approach a body of water, however small, in the dark. He needed to make certain that the water hole was not contaminated or that a predator was not already using the oasis.

James slept until the sun was fairly high in the sky, and then gathered up and secured the packs on the mules and began his trek to find water. He traveled a good part of the day, stopping at various promising compressions where moisture could be smelled. James worried that he had been precipitous in doling out his last reserves of water that morning to calm the animals and wondered if the sense of moisture was misleading. It took five or six frustrated stops to find a moist depression in the ground where a little digging would produce a small pool of water. He brought the horses one by one to the hole, and then the mules, to drink. It took minutes after each animal for the small hole to again fill with water and for James to finally drink his own fill. It didn't matter that the water was brackish and tasted like alkaline; it was a godsend.

James continued west until he found the main stream of the Carson River. He followed this river for days upon days until he finally entered into Eagle Valley next to the Sierra Nevada Mountains. James followed the Carson River to the edge of these wondrous and still snow-capped mountains where he came upon a ranch owned by the Hall brothers. The two brothers named Frank and W. L. Hall greeted him openly and invited James to sojourn with them while he and his animals rested. The Hall brothers were Mormons who had come to this part of the Utah Territory at the direction of their leader Brigham Young to settle the area and to provide supplies to the travelers on their way to California. They informed James that they—along with fellow Mormons Frank and Joseph Bernard, George Follensbee, and A. J. Rollins—intended to open a trading post to accomplish this mission. This trading post would become the Eagle Station Trading Post, named for an eagle shot by Frank Hall with his cap-and-ball Colt, and would ultimately be named Carson City, again after scout Kit Carson.

James stayed on the Hall brothers' ranch for three days while the animals grazed on good grass, drank clear water, and replenished their energy. James was grateful for the company of the brothers, as well as George Follensbee who worked on the ranch, although there was some proselytizing for their Mormon faith. James was not one to give his faith to any other entity but himself, and so the efforts of the men fell on deaf ears. This did not seem to diminish the goodwill of the Halls or Follensbee in giving James all of the supplies for which he could trade. Indeed, James was able to trade much of Jed Belleau's goods, as well as one horse and two mules, to the men for food and nugget gold. James was glad to be rid of Belleau's loot and felt that the last encumbrance of Jed Belleau was now gone.

The summer was quickly nearing its end, and James was keen to get over the mountains before the first snowfall. Frank Hall rode with James a ways to show him the way to Kit Carson Pass, a journey traversed by present-day State Route 88 in Alpine County, California. The pass was named for his scout by John C. Fremont in 1844. In January of that year, Fremont and his expedition were returning from the Pacific coast of Oregon on their way to the Rockies and had camped in what was to become the Carson Valley. Snow was falling and supplies were low. Fremont realized they would not make it through to the Rockies without resupplying, and Kit Carson suggested they head back west to Sutter's Fort where they could replenish their supplies. Local Washoe Indians told them of a route through the Sierra Nevada Mountains south of present-day Lake Tahoe but warned them not to do it in the snow. The expedition ignored the advice and proceeded across the mountains anyway. To their chagrin, they were unable to find food or game and they ultimately resorted to eating their dogs, horses, and mules just to survive.

On February 14, 1844, Fremont made it up Red Lake Peak and became the first white man to see Lake Tahoe. Seven days later, the expedition made it through what Fremont named Kit Carson Pass just west of Red Lake and, on March 6, arrived at Sutter's Fort with all intact. Five years later, a group of Mormons built a wagon trail through Kit Carson Pass all the way to present-day Carson Valley. This route became known as the Carson Trail and was the most popular of the wagon train routes for the forty-niners who wanted to work in the northern mines.

As James Vanderlin stood atop the summit of Kit Carson Pass looking down upon the gold fields of California, he noticed a tree that had an inscription carved by Kit Carson those six years earlier. Beneath the carving was nailed a cowhide from an animal that had been butchered along the trail. James was suddenly struck with a notion of how his future fortune would be made in California.

CHAPTER 17

Elko (Present Day)

Elizabeth Ryder sat in the dining room of the bed-and-breakfast on Silver Street. She had a bagel with cream cheese on a plate before her. She sat there looking down at the bagel, staring at it but not touching it. They were all there, the boarders except Izzy, eating their continental breakfast while waiting to be interviewed by Detective Dillon and Officer Neubrander. No one knew exactly where Izzy was, but all thought that she was probably sedated in her room. Elizabeth had no appetite. The events of the day before had sapped any desire for conviviality. Jason sat next to Elizabeth but seemed to have no problem eating his cereal and pastry. Vincent Lowler walked around the table pouring coffee into cups and placing them in front of his patrons. All were somber, and there was little conversation at the table.

Michelle Neubrander sat at the makeshift table in the salon, a card table from the basement of the bed-and-breakfast, waiting for Frank Dillon to begin his interviews. Frank stood at the painting of Eli Wilkes, staring at the painting and stroking his chin with the fingers of his right hand, his left hand securing his right elbow above his waist. He seemed lost in thought, yet his eyes roved over the picture, noticing every detail, every paint stroke. Michelle wondered what he was doing but did not ask. She waited instead. After a few moments, Frank turned from the painting and sat at the table next to Michelle.

"As you suggested, we'll start with Ed Walch," Frank began. "I will ask questions, and I would like you to take notes. I would like you to write as much of what they say as you can, exactly as they say it. We're not in a hurry, so if you need me to slow down, or them, or to go back, just say so. I am going to tape it as well. The reason I want you to take notes is that it takes forever to get the tapes transcribed, and we need something to work with long before that. Also, it takes a long time to go through transcripts once they are done. We'll use the transcripts mostly for verification, but we will work from notes. When we are not together, take notes on what you are doing. I will do the same. We'll go over our notes when we get back together. The notes are important because every day, at the end of our day, we will be writing reports on all of our activities. The notes will be our memory. Questions?"

Michelle shook her head and withdrew a tablet of paper from her bag next to her chair. Michelle was dressed in civilian clothes, a white blouse tucked into light brown slacks. She wore flat dark brown shoes—comfortable shoes that matched her waist-length jacket in color. Her forty-caliber Smith and Wesson semiautomatic handgun rested in her bag along with two additional bullet magazines, her handcuffs, and her hang badge. She wore a medium wide brown belt around her slacks in case she had to put her equipment on in a hurry. She didn't sleep well the night before, waiting for the phone call from her sergeant, which came at six in the morning, informing her that she would be working with Frank on this case. Frank had told her the night before to wear comfortable clothes that wouldn't intimidate those whom they would interview. A uniform, as Michelle was keenly aware, naturally drew a kind of response from people, whether respectful consideration, uncomfortable intimidation, or resentful resistance. Frank wanted to eliminate that factor in his attempt to gain information.

Ed Walch sat in the chair in front of them with an immediate affable comfort. He seemed actually to be enjoying the process. This bode well in the minds of both Frank and Michelle. Someone who looked forward to being interviewed by the police in a homicide investigation was an unlikely killer. Or he might be a total sociopath who enjoyed the contest with the inquisitors. This was less likely in Frank's experience. Although most of the sociopaths that Frank had encountered in his career had little or no guilt over their misdeeds, they also had no desire to suffer the consequences of their actions. Few of them had succumbed to murder, having limited their unscrupulous behaviors to wreaking dysfunction to the point of devastation in their families and associates.

Ed seemed more the type of person who liked to peek at that devastation rather than experience it. He was the gawker along the freeway at the site of a terrible accident, not the one who caused it. He enjoyed watching the play, not acting in it. However, in this situation, he was a spectator who had important information to share. He had been one of the first to see the body of Benjamin and, in his mind, had been the one to take charge after the call for the police and in securing the room from tampering. He had seen this done in movies and believed that he had done well. It was now time for his accolades from the professionals. Throughout the questioning, Ed brought the material back to the fact that he had been the one to keep everyone from disturbing the scene and the available evidence. Before the end of the interview, Frank made sure to compliment Ed on his handling of the first moments of discovering Benjamin's body, much to Michelle's astonishment and chagrin. She did not like Ed Walch, thinking him narrow, self-important, and pompous. She meant to ask Frank after the interview why he was so solicitous to such an unlikable individual but ultimately forgot about it.

Ed's version of the events of the night before differed little from Izzy's. When questioned about his activities prior to dinner that day, Ed recounted that he had gone to the Stockmen's Casino, in the company of Elizabeth and Jason Ryder, to gamble. He had stayed there approximately two hours but had left after losing his allotted thirty dollars and had gone back to his room to read. Right after lunch, he had seen Benjamin Dulles going down the stairs to the basement where Vincent Lowler had his rooms, but that was the last time he had seen Benjamin alive. He had never met Benjamin or Izzy Dulles before this vacation even though he was related to them through James Vanderlin's sister, and he knew of no one who would have wanted Benjamin dead. He could not account for the activities of anyone other than Elizabeth and Jason in the hours between lunch and that fateful dinner.

After Ed Walch, Frank interviewed Elizabeth Ryder, who corroborated Ed Walch's version of the after-lunch-before-dinner events of the previous day concerning the Stockmen's Casino foray. The only difference between Ed's and Elizabeth's recollections of the previous day was that Elizabeth could only corroborate Ed at the Stockmen's Casino for the first hour there, but not after that. Also, she remembered it being Marvin Cosgrove who took charge after the discovery of Benjamin's murder. Elizabeth, as well, had never met anyone at the bed-and-breakfast prior to this week, excepting Jason of course, even though being related to most of them through James Vanderlin's younger sister. She liked Izzy very much and, because of Izzy, liked Benjamin. She thought him odd in a pathetic sort of way but understood him somewhat through Izzy. She saw Benjamin as being harmless and couldn't imagine why anyone would want to kill him. Elizabeth had not seen Benjamin at all that previous day and had not seen anything out of the ordinary that could shed light on the tragedy.

After interviewing Marvin Cosgrove then Jason Ryder, Marjorie Cosgrove, and Andy Walsh, they broke for lunch at twelve thirty. Frank and Michelle drove through the McDonald's restaurant drive-through on Idaho Street and ate their lunch in the unmarked police car, sitting at the park behind the Northeastern Nevada Museum. Frank wanted to go over Michelle's notes while they ate, and he didn't want anyone overhearing their conversation. Frank complimented Michelle on the completeness of her notes and gave suggestions on mind-cue shortcuts that would help with the flow of the notes.

Reviewing the interviews, they decided that the most relevant information to come out so far was that Ed Walch had seen Benjamin Dulles going downstairs to the basement. This had been corroborated by Marjorie Cosgrove who had been sitting on the steps waiting for Marvin to finish his conversation with Izzy in the dining room, and Benjamin had passed by her on his way to the basement. Vincent Lowler had an apartment made up of two rooms in the basement, including a kitchen/living-room/office combination and a bedroom with a toilet and shower at one end. There was also a storage room and a furnace room in the basement. Off to the side of the storage room was a coal bin and chute that went up concrete steps to the side yard. They decided they would interview Vincent Lowler first after lunch to find out if Benjamin had descended the stairs to speak to him, and then they would interview Edna Wahl, the cook; Francie Benniger, the housekeeper; and Juan Ortiz, the dishwasher/gardener, thereafter.

The interview with Vincent Lowler revealed that Benjamin had indeed come down to the basement to speak to him. Vincent stated that Benjamin wanted to know more about the painting in the salon: had it always been in the house, or had it been purchased somewhere else and brought there? Benjamin wanted to know what Vincent had done in his renovation of the house—whether he had renovated the entire house, and if not, what was not renovated. Also, how long had Vincent owned the house, from whom had he purchased it, and where might the previous owners be now? Vincent found the questions tedious and felt that Benjamin was being obsessive, but he did not say so to Benjamin. He tried to be patient and answer the questions as best he could. As far as he knew, the painting had always been in the house from the time of its creation. He had renovated to achieve his apartment and to bring the rest of the house in compliance with what he could discern of that past time. He did not change the structure of the house but only the cosmetic surface. And yes, he realized that he was probably the last one to see Benjamin alive other than the killer.

Vincent had purchased the house from Bill and Betty Friedman seven years previous. They had operated it as a bed-and-breakfast establishment but had not tried to do it as a period place. They had used the top floor as their apartment, leaving less room for guests, and tried to do the cooking and cleaning themselves. They had done very little to embellish the historical significance of the painting to the house to make it a destination vacation place. It turned out to be too much work and did not make enough money to sustain them as they wished. Vincent had stayed there one time and saw the possibilities of what it could become. His father had died leaving him some disposable cash, and he jumped at the chance to operate his own business, one where he could work and live at the same time. He was happy here and made enough money to make it all worthwhile.

Frank questioned Vincent on what Vincent knew about the painting and its claim of being the pathway to riches. Vincent indicated that he knew the stories about the Vanderlin gold but really didn't believe them. As far as he was concerned, the painting was a gimmick to get people to want to stay in his inn. He hoped there was no gold or, if there was, that it stayed hidden until he was done living his dream of being an independent business owner. In any case, if there was gold, he didn't believe it would be found in his house. No, he hadn't really looked for it, other than to pay attention during the renovation just in case. He found Benjamin's obsession with the gold somewhat irritating only in the sense that it irritated his other guests. Otherwise, he didn't care one way or another what Benjamin did or thought.

The interviews of the cook, housekeeper, and dishwasher/gardener brought very little new information to the investigation. They had paid little attention to Benjamin Dulles at any time and did not notice him on that particular day. They were busy with their duties and saw nothing out of the normal. The housekeeper, Francie Benniger, had made up Benjamin's room during breakfast but did not notice anything out of the ordinary. Little had changed in the room from the previous day, and she could not attest to anything being missing from the room.

The last interview of the day was Izzy again. Michelle had gone upstairs and roused Izzy from her bed, where she had been asleep with the help of medications prescribed by the physician the night before. Her breakfast and lunch had been brought up to the room by Edna Wahl but had been left untouched on the dresser. Frank decided to come up to Izzy's room to do the interview as Michelle reported how groggy Izzy was when she awakened Izzy. Frank brought a folding chair with him and sat next to the bed where Izzy lay. Michelle sat in the soft chair opposite the dresser, taking notes.

"Izzy, do you remember if Bennie said anything about this house or the people in it?" Frank prodded gently. "Do you think it is possible that Bennie discovered something, maybe about the gold or about someone here, that might have scared someone? Did he say anything at all?"

Izzy sat against the headboard trying to focus her eyes and her thoughts. She looked a mess. Her hair hadn't been washed in two days and had been slept on for almost that long. Her face was drawn and pale, and her body seemed deflated on the bed. She wore the same clothes as the day before, which were rumpled and seemed carelessly thrown on. She was simply in disarray and acted defeated, lost.

"Are you asking if Bennie found the treasure?" she asked listlessly. Frank did not respond, but waited. "I don't know. I don't think so," Izzy continued. "He would have been excited if he had found anything like that. I can't imagine what he would have found about anyone else that would have made anyone do this. Bennie didn't care that much about people to be interested in them or what they had done. He wasn't like that. People just didn't interest him that much, and if he had found out something, he wouldn't have done anything with it. He didn't care about that kind of thing."

"Did you notice if anything was missing from Bennie's room?" Frank asked.

"No," Izzy responded. "I didn't look. But I don't think Bennie had anything that anyone would want to steal. Nothing that I knew of anyway."

Frank nodded and rose to his feet.

"Thank you, Izzy," he said, picking up the folding chair. "We will leave you to get some sleep." He said this as he nodded to Michelle to leave.

"Wait," Izzy spoke faintly. "I want to take Bennie back to Michigan to bury him. When can I take him?"

"Just as soon as the medical examiner is done with him. It shouldn't be more than a day or two, then you can go."

Izzy rolled over onto her side even before Frank and Michelle had stepped out of the room. She appeared to drift immediately back into sleep. Michelle closed the door behind them.

CHAPTER 18

San Francisco (1859)

James Vanderlin stood atop the wheelhouse of the two-masted wooden boat afloat in the harbor of San Francisco Bay. He was watching the lights of many torches bobbing up and down on the docks several hundred yards away. The ship on which he stood had been in this spot since he had arrived in San Francisco seven years ago. The ship had been abandoned by its crew in 1851 when all aboard left for the gold fields near Coloma hoping to gain their fortunes. James was in Coloma then, determined that he would move his operation from Coloma and Sacramento to San Francisco. He accomplished this later that same year.

After crossing the Sierra Nevada Mountains into the California gold fields in the fall of 1850, James began buying the hides of all the cattle that were being butchered to provide food to the settlers and miners. He paid little for these hides as most would have been discarded as useless. James hired Chinese, Mexican, and Indian workers to clean, tan, and work the hides into leather goods such as gloves, leggings, and aprons for the miners. The workers, who had predominately come to the gold fields to get rich themselves but had faced severe discrimination and hardships from the white population of miners, turned out to be industrious and cheap labor.

Although James began his leather goods industry in Coloma, nearest the gold fields, he expanded quickly to Hangtown (later Placerville) and Sacramento. Considering the low cost of materials and labor, James immediately began expanding his wealth as the miners, many of whom came unprepared for the intense physical labor involved in removing gold from the streams and then the dirt banks of rivers, were willing to pay exorbitant prices for these basic goods. James made it his practice to be at the sites of these labors with his wares immediately available. He hired more and more men—men who would not be easily robbed or taken in by the sad stories of the hopeless dreamers—to sell his leather goods at the gold sites. He paid these men better wages than that offered by mine owners or robber captains.

As James's wealth increased, he expanded his enterprises beyond dealing in leather goods. James became the hidden, silent partner in a money-loaning business where the legitimate, out-front partner needed someone with James's skill to collect the moneys owed. Many of the men James had hired to sell and protect his leather goods and money now became useful in this new enterprise, strong-arming the unfortunate who had borrowed against hope. It was through this business that James and his financial partner became the owners of two prospering gold claims, both of which the previous owners, it was rumored, had given up their claims in fear of their lives.

Thus, by 1852, James was able to move his offices and residence to the two-masted boat in the harbor of San Francisco Bay. Taking over ownership of the boat had been no problem as James simply threw out the squatters who inhabited the ship and, by hanging their leader from the timbers in the bowels of the boat, insured their silence and their promise to never return. He chose this ship because of its location in the harbor, the fact that it was free-floating and in fairly good condition, and the fact that it was technically no longer owned by anyone. The only approach to the ship was by water, and thus it was easily defended. James was not interested in a public venue to do business, as that was his partner's position, and since the only people with whom James intended to have contact with on the boat were those who were willing and needed to journey to the ship by skiff.

James Vanderlin had again built an underground enterprise just under the surface from a legitimate business whose goal was the accumulation of wealth by nefarious means. His organization was mirrored on the criminal enterprise he had built back in Peoria when he was engineering Josie's happiness and was ostensibly a police officer. James was still interested in appearing legitimate, but it was not his nature to wait for the slow accumulation of wealth that a legitimate business offered. He wanted it all, and he wanted it now. Thus, his legitimate enterprises expanded through intimidation, extortion, and sometimes, murder.

By the fall of 1858, James had outmaneuvered his partner by secretly murdering his partner's wife and introducing his subsequently grieving partner to the escape of opium. The opium was supplied in needed quantities by James's Chinese leather-goods workers. It was a simple step to then move his partner out of the business and into the arms of a prostitute who claimed to be the widow of a Baptist minister. James settled the partner and his prostitute wife into a small leather goods shop in the Barbary Coast section of San Francisco, where the partner quickly succumbed to a lethal dose of opium and the prostitute wife transformed the shop into her own bordello. The prostitute wife and James thereafter formed their own kind of partnership, which gave each a unique kind of information and intelligence on the activities of the surrounding Barbary Coast.

In January of 1859, gold was discovered at the head of Six-Mile Canyon on Mount Davidson outside of Carson City in the Utah Territory by two miners named McLaughlin and O'Reilly. Another miner, Henry Comstock, came upon them and convinced McLaughlin and O'Reilly that their discovery was on Comstock's claim. Unfortunately for them, they believed Comstock, and so began one of the most important gold-and-silver discoveries in the west, claimed of course by Henry Comstock. More gold was discovered that same month in Gold Canyon on Mount Davidson by James Finney, or Old Virginny as he was known because of his birthplace. James Finney was not the sharpest of men and soon sold his claim for fifty dollars. However, the town that grew up around the gold discovered on Mount Davidson became known as Virginia City, named after hapless Old Virginny.

James Vanderlin was keenly interested in Virginia City and its gold discoveries. He had traveled through the Carson Valley in 1850 when it was known as Eagle Valley, and he was familiar with the area. He remembered the Carson River and how he had felt finally reaching its oasis after his perilous journey through the Forty-Mile Desert, and so had a fondness for the region. News of the Comstock Lode discovery quickly reached the Barbary Coast of San Francisco and, through the prostitute wife's bordello, to James's ears. James quickly organized his resources to bring his leather goods to Virginia City and to the miners there. James himself traveled to Virginia City three times during the year of 1859 to set up his leather goods business in that area, employing some of the failed Chinese miners at the Comstock Lode to produce the leather from the cowhides he bought in the Carson Valley.

The year 1859 was cataclysmic for James in San Francisco. He had taken over a saloon in the Barbary Coast section of San Francisco in the fall of 1858 when the saloon owner could not make good on the usury interest James had charged on a money loan. The man had made noisy protests over the hidden costs James assessed on the loan and was subsequently found floating face down in the San Francisco Bay with a knife in his back. This became an unfortunate public scandal for James, who had anticipated the currents and sharks in the bay disposing of the evidence of the misdeed. Then, in the spring of 1859, the brother of the Catholic archbishop of San Francisco was stabbed to death in the alley behind the saloon after welching on a bet at one of the faro tables in the saloon. During the summer of that year, the mayor's daughter was found prostituting her body for money in the upstairs of the saloon. It was rumored that she had become addicted to opium in the basement of that very establishment at her eighteenth birthday celebration and was touted as the "celebrity" prostitute by the saloon's management to those that were interested in that sort of activity, much to the chagrin of the mayor and the city's aristocracy.

Finally, in October of 1859, one Jacob Isaac Berentsen had come to the saloon to celebrate his wedding to young Rebecca Brandt, which had occurred just down the street on Pacific Avenue. Jacob, beginning the next morning, was to work in Rebecca's father's bank off Nob Hill in San Francisco and was to ultimately run the bank. Jacob and Rebecca and some of their young friends sat at a table near one of the faro tables. After several drinks, Jacob, who had never played faro before, decided he would try his luck at the game. Unfortunately for the faro dealer, or *banker* as he was called, Jacob was incredibly observant where money was concerned—which made him invaluable in his father-in-law's bank—and noticed that the banker was burning off two soda cards, one under the other, instead of the legal one. He loudly interrupted the play and accused the banker of cheating.

A fight broke out amongst patrons and employees and, somehow, Jacob ended up at the top of the stairs to the second-floor balcony ferociously sparring with two large men who worked for the saloon. The two men got the best of Jacob and lifted him up over the rail to the balcony. As they shoved Jacob over the balcony, Rebecca screamed and ran under the balcony to break Jacob's twenty-five-foot fall to the wooden floor below. Jacob fell on Rebecca, breaking her neck and killing her instantly. When their friends rolled Jacob off Rebecca, they found a knife sticking out of his chest. The two men at the top of the stairs had subsequently disappeared.

This was the final straw for the good people of San Francisco, and on that night in October of 1859, a crowd gathered on the wharf at San Francisco Bay, torches blazing and voices loud and menacing. James Vanderlin stood on the wheelhouse of the boat, watching the crowd gather on the wharf. He had been advised of the incident at the saloon and had been moving his important things from the ship into two small boats tied to the side of the ship opposite the wharf. He couldn't sail the ship out of the bay because he had never taken the time, nor had the inclination, to learn how. The ship was simply his home and office, and he had never actually thought of it in any other way.

Standing on the wheelhouse, watching the crowd as they began climbing into small boats, James had no illusions about the outcome of this night. He was done in San Francisco and was no longer welcome there. It was of little consequence to James in terms of his businesses since he had begun moving his enterprises to Virginia City in the Utah Territory that very year. Even so, it was not how James wanted to be perceived. He wanted—needed—the appearance of respectability. This was not how he intended his departure from San Francisco to be. He didn't need to be hailed as a king or thought of as a saint. But respectability had been nailed to his armor by his father those many years ago and, while his nature prohibited its actual accomplishment, he needed the appearance nonetheless. It was the one attribute, the one legacy of his father that he could not shake loose.

As the boats carrying the torchbearers began leaving the wharf, moving slowly toward James's ship, James climbed down the rope ladder to one of the waiting skiffs below. Four men sat at the oars, two of the men being the very same as had knifed poor Jacob Berentsen some hours before, and began rowing the skiff into the night toward a farther point in the harbor. There a carriage awaited James, already loaded with his valuable items, to take him to his new paradise. James turned in the carriage as it moved up the hill and watched the steady ship that he had called home for the past seven years burn into the water of the bay.

CHAPTER 19

Elko (Present Day)

Elizabeth and Jason were crossing Third Street from the post office at the west end of Commercial Street. They had walked to the post office from the bed-and-breakfast on Silver Street one block south and four blocks east and were intending to stop for breakfast at the Stockmen's Casino on Commercial Street. Jason was chattering as he walked about the recent events and how he had always wanted to be part of a murder investigation, although he wished they were privy to more information about the investigation. He realized that they, he and Elizabeth, were peripheral to the investigation and were not deserving of inclusion in the process, yet the entire concept was exciting to him. It made him think that perhaps he would become a police officer, that perhaps that was his true calling.

Jason glanced at Elizabeth to see if she was listening since she had given no indication through his recitation that she had even heard. Her look was somber and very distant.

"Liz?" Jason queried. "Did you hear me? Are you all right?"

Elizabeth started as if she was brought back to this place from somewhere else.

"I'm sorry, Jason," she responded. "I did hear what you were saying, and if you want to be a police officer, I think that is great." She said this as they were walking into the Stockmen's Casino. He continued the conversation after they had been seated for breakfast in the café.

"What is going on, Liz?" Jason inquired.

"What do you mean?" Elizabeth asked too quickly, defensively.

"You're not here. When I talk to you, it's like you are someplace else. What's wrong?"

Elizabeth dropped her eyes, concentrating on the menu. She finally looked up.

"I don't know. I guess I just feel bad for Izzy. You know she left this morning to take Bennie back to Michigan. I feel like I should have done something, said something. We'll never see her again, and it just ended so badly. I mean . . . Izzy has lost everything. It's like her life is over, and I didn't know what to do. I felt like we kind of made a connection, and I should have done more!"

"What could you have done?" Jason asked sincerely.

"I don't know, Jason," Elizabeth answered. "Something—anything! After that thing happened to Bennie, I didn't speak to her again."

Jason started to protest but stopped when Elizabeth held up her hand.

"I know what you are going to say," she commented. "I know it is not my fault—what happened. But you saw Izzy, it was like she was completely done for. She is all alone! She has to go through this all alone! I feel like I should have done something to help her. At least say something to her before she left!"

"Like what?" Jason asked.

Elizabeth was becoming more animated, almost angry. "I don't know! Maybe let her know that it will get better with time. Something along that line, something to give her hope. It was as if all hope had been taken away from her. It's like she has nothing more to live for. I am afraid for her!"

Jason nodded but didn't say anything. Just then, the waitress came up to take their order. Jason, ever the prepared one, knew exactly what he wanted. Elizabeth just ordered coffee. He noticed Detective Dillon and Officer Neubrander enter the café and look in their direction. Jason nudged Elizabeth under the table as Dillon and Neubrander came up to their table.

"Hey, folks," Detective Dillon said as he came to stand in front of their booth. "Would you mind if we sat with you?"

"Not at all," Elizabeth stated, moving over for him to sit down. Michelle Neubrander slid in next to Jason.

"What's good?" Frank inquired.

Both Jason and Elizabeth simply shrugged.

"I guess I'll just have coffee," Frank addressed the waitress who walked up with the coffee urn. Michelle followed suit. The waitress was back in a few minutes with Jason's 'biscuits and gravy with eggs' breakfast.

"How is the investigation going?" Elizabeth asked. "Have you found out anything? Do you have any idea who did this?"

Frank shook his head as he sipped the coffee. "Not much yet, but it is still early." He ignored the last question.

"I heard Izzy left this morning," Elizabeth continued. "Did you talk to her before she left? Was she doing any better?"

"We put her on the plane to Salt Lake City. She'll switch there for Michigan," Frank responded.

"Elizabeth feels bad for Izzy," Jason explained between mouthfuls. "She thinks she should have done something to help her."

Elizabeth gave him a withering look across the table.

Frank turned to Elizabeth with surprise. "What should you have done?" he asked.

Elizabeth had the cornered look of the prey and would have kicked her brother under the table if it hadn't been so obvious. She collected her thoughts before answering.

"She just seemed so lost," Elizabeth began. "She seemed like a hurt child. I know that she was in pain and wanted to be alone in her room, but I felt like I should have been able to do something to comfort her. I couldn't think of anything to say or do, so I did nothing."

Frank smiled a sympathetic smile. "I understand," he acknowledged. "But she was on some pretty significant medication for those days, and I doubt that anything you could have said or done would have made much of a difference. One thing I have learned in my career is that there are certain hurts that no one can take from you, no one can relieve you of. You have to go through them alone, and the only thing that works is when someone is simply there when you need them. It's not what you say or do, it's simply being there. It comes down to this—Izzy is in Michigan, and you are here. When she finally realizes she needs someone to be there, it will have to be someone in Michigan."

"Does she have anyone there?" Jason asked, pushing the emptied plate away. "It sounded to me like Bennie was her whole world. Are there any other relatives? Do you know of any friends?"

"We asked if there was anyone," Michelle answered, speaking for the first time. "She simply said that she would be all right and not to be concerned about her. She probably has a group of friends that will take care of her if there are no other relatives."

"What about the murder?" Elizabeth persisted. "Are there any clues about who did this?"

Frank smiled his most patronizing smile. "We really can't discuss the investigation or comment on any one person. However, if you are up to a question or two—and let me emphasize that the questions we ask are simply to get information, most probably for background and are not to be construed as implying a specific person is a murderer or is involved in a crime—"

"Shoot." Jason answered Frank's smile with his own.

Frank nodded to Michelle.

"What do you think of Vincent Lowler?" she queried, opening her notebook. Michelle automatically addressed this question to Elizabeth, ignoring Jason.

Elizabeth paused thoughtfully then answered, "He seems very bright, but narrow."

Frank cocked his head attentively. "Narrow?" he asked.

"Yes," Elizabeth explained, turning her attention from Michelle to Frank. "He doesn't say much, mostly just hovers. I get the feeling that he hears everything but really doesn't add anything to whatever is being said except when he is asked directly. Then he always seems to have an answer. It's as if he is on reserve. I think he knows a lot more than he offers but acts like he is not interested." She paused again for a moment, considering. "Actually, he reminds me a lot of Bennie—like his interest is very directed."

"Directed toward what?" Frank asked.

"Well, he seems to be interested only in business and money," Elizabeth answered. "He will talk freely about the bed-and-breakfast and how much money he makes or can make or what he is planning on doing to increase business. But if you bring the subject to James Vanderlin's gold, which does have to do with the house and his business, he seems to have little to say, or he says things that just stop the conversation. It's like he dismisses the stories so strongly that it does no good to talk about it in front of him. Yet he is always around, listening."

"Interesting," Frank commented. "What do you think of him, Jason?"

Jason smiled. "I think he is a goof," he said softly. "He lives and breathes that place, like it's some kind of shrine."

"What about Andy Walch?" Michelle asked Elizabeth. "What are your thoughts about him?"

Elizabeth laughed. "Andy is like a big kid. He's not stupid or anything, he just doesn't care about anything—except eating."

"I understand he didn't come upstairs with the rest of you when you found Benjamin?" Frank asked.

"That's right, he didn't," Jason responded.

"Do you know why?" Michelle took up the question. "What was he doing?"

Jason looked at Elizabeth, as if looking for help. Her glance back was equally confused.

"I don't know," Elizabeth responded. "I didn't think about it at the time. The rest of us were all there or on the stairs. But I don't think Andy came out of the dining room."

"What did he say he was doing?" Jason asked.

"Ahhh!" Frank responded. "That's the question. He says he doesn't remember but thinks he was on the stairs with everyone else. Yet no one remembers him being there."

Elizabeth shook her head as if searching for a lost memory. "No, I'm pretty sure he wasn't there."

"What do you think of Ed Walch?" Michelle's question was directed to Elizabeth again. However, it was Jason who answered.

"A blowhard!" he declared. He then looked up and realized everyone was looking at him, waiting. "He's a talker, a know-it-all. I doubt he's done half the things he claims. He's always trying to impress."

Elizabeth grinned as Michelle nodded in obvious agreement.

"And the Cosgroves?" Michelle continued.

"They seem nice," Jason responded again. Then he glanced at Elizabeth with an impish grin. "Liz thinks they are the picture of love."

Elizabeth turned red but stayed quiet.

"Is that so?" Frank asked.

"I just think it is sweet when two people who have been married as long as they treat each other with deference and respect and, yes, love," she challenged Jason. "It's not so common, you know," Elizabeth said this defensively to Frank and Michelle.

Frank nodded as Michelle just stared at Elizabeth.

"So it isn't," he declared absently. "So it isn't."

He looked across at Michelle.

"Well, Michelle, are you ready to go?"

Michelle nodded and put her notebook back into her bag. They rose together and nodded to Jason and Elizabeth.

"See you later," Frank said.

"Wait!" Elizabeth cried. "When will we be able to go home?"

Frank stopped and pondered. "Soon," he said and left the café with Michelle in tow.

CHAPTER 20

Virginia City (1860)

James Vanderlin woke with a start. Something was wrong! The room was dark, but he could discern the curtains moving in the breeze. The window was open! Had he left it open when he went to bed? Yes, he thought it was possible that he had. His room in the hotel was large but sparsely furnished. His bed was in the center of the room with its high headboard of heavy mahogany. On the other side of the headboard, against the wall, was a white-painted iron claw-footed bathtub. It weighed four hundred pounds and had to stand on a reinforced wooden platform to distribute the weight from its legs. Next to it was a small table with soaps, a crystal decanter of water, and a washbasin. On the other side of the bed at the far end of the room was placed a plush easy chair under a gas lamp that extended from the wall. A large ornately carved wardrobe stood against the wall next to the door, and directly across the room from the wardrobe was the open window with its billowing curtains.

James heard a sound and sat upright in the bed. It sounded vague, like an exhaled sigh or a soft swoosh of air. He began to turn on the bed to look behind the headboard when the last of the available light suddenly disappeared. A burlap bag was forced over his head, and his arms were pinned by large rough hands. James was wrestled to the floor as the bag was secured below his neck, and a rope was tied around his head forcing his jaws and mouth open. He could not speak or utter any intelligible sounds. Rope was wrapped around his arms and wrists and tied tightly. James was then hoisted to his feet and dragged across the floor to the door. He could hear the movement of several men—large men, he guessed by the sounds—as they moved to the door and stopped for a moment, listening. A few quiet moments later, they opened the door and hustled him down the hall to the backdoor and the stairs at the back of the building.

Outside, James could feel the cool night breeze as it whispered up the stairs and whistled slightly through the eaves above him. It was a pleasant feeling and sound, absurdly so considering his situation. James tried to count the number of men based on their sounds and believed there were at least four. They marched him down the stairs in the alleyway and thrust him over the pommel of a horse. A man climbed up behind him and urged the horse to motion. James lay across the pommel of the saddle on his stomach thinking how uncomfortable he was and hoping they would not ride far. His mind was busy assessing his predicament and calculating his odds of escape. Without being able to remove the bag from his head, without being able to see what was happening, James considered his chances of escape to be minimal.

It was not unexpected that he would be found in this condition. After arriving in Virginia City over a year ago, James had set about establishing himself in the town. He had taken a room in the hotel, the one from which he had just been taken, and had begun improving his financial situation. He sold the two mines in California to some ventures from Australia just in time. The mines had begun to peter out of their gold, and it was becoming harder and harder to extract the gold from the layers of earth. The expense of more and greater placer mining for less and less gold was taking its toll on James's resources, and he had neither the patience nor the inclination to see it through. He made a tidy profit on the mines but kept the saloon in the Barbary Coast area of San Francisco. He paid a man of similar nature to James to run the place and to keep him informed of all that was worth knowing in San Francisco. He paid the man very well, better than any other nearby establishment, knowing that although he could not buy the man's honesty, trust, or loyalty, he could certainly own his time and energy. He secretly paid other men and women who worked in the saloon to keep tabs on the manager. It was expensive on James's part, but experience had taught him that it was worth the money to keep an account of people. He almost always knew when someone was stealing from him with a minimal amount of investigation and without having to be there.

After arriving in Virginia City, James looked to his primary and legitimate source of income: his leather goods business. He knew that he would always have the upper hand when it came to supplying leather goods to the miners because his goods were made on-site, and he cut out the middlemen, the retailers. Additionally, his labor was cheap because he utilized the failed Chinese miners and railroad workers who could not find other employment. He could afford to sell his products to the miners for less money than the local mercantile stores, and in some cases, his gloves and leather accessories could be tailored to the individual. This, of course, did not make him popular with the store owners who sold comparable goods. But then this never bothered James. The distressful plight of others was never in the forefront of James's consideration unless it somehow furthered his ambitions.

Of course, there were James's other enterprises as well. He brought opium to Virginia City through his Chinese workers and bought a saloon on the edge of town to encourage this trade. The entrance to his saloon on E Street, very near the cemetery, opened into the drinking and gambling arena where faro tables occupied the wall opposite the long, exquisitely fashioned wood bar with its ceiling high mirrored back wall. He imported prostitutes with the help of his partner, the prostitute wife in the Barbary Coast of San Francisco, and had them ply their trade in the four rooms in the upstairs of the saloon. The bottom floor of the saloon, essentially the basement, was carved out of the hillside with a door opening onto an alleyway above F Street. This door, which allowed access out of but not into the building, was the exit from the basement opium den established on that bottom floor.

James had accomplished all of this in a little over a year. In addition, James had made it a point to know all of Virginia City's nefarious characters—if not in person, certainly in reputation. He had his men, who had come to Virginia City with him, make contacts with these individuals in case he needed them in the future. His own men consisted of the three that he had brought from San Francisco, including the two who had knifed Jacob Berentsen in October of 1859. He had accumulated these men from those that he had employed in California to guard his money and leather goods in the gold fields in the early 1850s, and these three especially he paid well to keep their respect and fidelity. He had convinced them over the years that they would profit from their continued association with him. And with them he could truly be himself: that is, he didn't have to feign respectability.

The horse across whose pommel James was trussed finally stopped. James was roughly pulled from the horse and thrown onto the ground. He could hear men tramping around him, alighting from horses, and could hear other men approaching on foot. James was lifted to a standing position, and the hood was cut and pulled from his head. The light of dawn was beginning to spring from atop the mountain as James shook his head to clear his vision. He counted seven men in the dawning light, the leader of whom was one of the shop owners that he had practically put out of business.

"What's this?" James demanded, his voice full and angry.

The shop owner, Lars Foley, approached to stand right in front of James, his face inches from James's face. He was at least six inches shorter, but he glared up at James, his face red with rage.

"You think you're something, don'cha—you and your high ways?" he blurted. "You think you can come into my town and start pushin' people around and we'll just stand for it! You don't fool us! You sell your stuff here, put other folks out of business, and walk around like you're something. Well, you're nothing! And in a few minutes, you're going to be less than nothing!"

James didn't respond but returned Foley's stare. Foley looked around, smugly taking in the faces of the other men with him, men of the nefarious character whom James had taken the trouble to cultivate.

"Do you know where you are?" Foley asked arrogantly, smirking.

James looked around at his surroundings. He shook his head slowly.

"You're at the bottom of Gold Canyon," Foley stated with a wicked smile. He nodded toward a gaping hole in the earth face to his left. "That's an old shaft that petered out. Inside, it drops forty feet straight down. Nobody goes there anymore."

"What are you getting at, Foley?" James asked impatiently.

Foley laughed a nervous laugh. "That's going to be your grave, you son of a bitch! Nobody is ever going to know what happened to you! You will just have disappeared—gone away! Not that anybody cares!"

"And who is going to do this? You?" James challenged.

"That's right!" Foley countered, surprised at James's impudence.

Foley didn't understand James's apparent lack of fear. Foley and some of the other shop owners had met and decided this course of action. They had seen through James's posture of respectability and believed him to be a parasite on the town's potential future. They didn't have the money to buy James out and didn't believe he would leave if they tried. James's saloon was becoming a problem, a blight on the community. Miners and other members of the community were being seduced by the women, the gambling, and the opium of the saloon, and it boded ill for the community. Yet none of it was illegal, which meant the constable would do nothing. In the end, it wasn't just the business. They simply didn't like James Vanderlin or the outright hypocrisy of his persona. He pretended to be a respectable person, a forthright businessman, but catered to the lowest in people and set about ruining others, including Foley, without conscience. This was the real crime, one about which the law would do nothing. This was why he and the other shop owners decided on this course, and Foley was the only one man enough to follow it through, to take the lead.
    "If I were you, I would start to make my peace with God!" Foley tried, less sure of his goal now.
    Vanderlin threw back his head and laughed a chilling, heart-piercing laugh.
    "Look around you, Foley," James ordered. "What do you see?"
    "What do you mean?" Foley asked, the chill of Vanderlin's laugh cocooning his heart, his knees beginning to feel weak. Foley looked around at the faces of the men behind and beside him. They were all looking at him like predators looking at prey. They were watching him, Foley thought, waiting to see what he would do. He had to take back control of this confrontation. He needed to be strong, decisive, and impressive. He had hired men who walked on the dark side of the law, intentionally so, and he needed to lead them, or they would not respect him, would not follow him. He needed to impress them!

"Get down on your knees and beg for your life!" he yelled at Vanderlin, his voice breaking slightly.

Again, James Vanderlin laughed—this time not so deeply, but more pityingly.

"You picked the wrong men, Foley!" James said softly. "These men work for me!"

James nodded to the two men on either side of Lars Foley, and they immediately grabbed Foley's arms in iron grips. A cry escaped Foley's lips as he tried to wrestle free from their grasp without success. The other men came forward and gathered around. A couple of them were obviously confused, not knowing what to do. James turned to them while a third man cut the ropes that bound his arms.

"You see, Bill and Andy here tried to extort money from me a while back at Devil's Gate when I was riding up to town from Gold Hill. I realized they were men that I could count on in a pinch, and we struck a deal. I gave them all my money that day and promised them double on top if they would help me when I needed it. And here we are! You men will find out that I pay better than anyone else in town, and anytime you work for me, you will get paid handsomely and quickly. Whatever Lars here agreed to pay you, I will double it right here and now!"

"But . . . but . . . !" Foley sputtered. "You men can't! You already agreed, and we already paid you!"

Several of the men laughed out loud as others snickered.

"What do you want us to do with him, boss?" the one named Bill asked.

James smiled maliciously.

"I think that we should follow the plan that he had for me," he responded with nods from the men. "It was a pretty good plan, considering."

"You'll never get away with this!" Foley managed to choke out, trembling. "People will miss me!"

"Probably," James quietly said. "But as you said, no one will know where you went. And believing is not proving! Take him over to the hole."

The men walked Lars Foley to the spent mine entrance and held him facing the hole while James came up behind him. James took the knife that Andy held in his hand, pulled Lars's head back by his hair, and cut his throat from side to side. He then pushed Foley into the mine and watched as he slid down the steep slope of the shaft to the vertical drop where he disappeared from view. Seconds later, they heard the sick thud as the body of Lars Foley hit the bottom of the mine shaft.

CHAPTER 21

Silver Street (Present Day)

Ed Walch fell down the third-floor stairs in the bed-and-breakfast house on Silver Street and broke his neck. That is not what he died from though. The Coroner found that the back of Ed's head had been bashed in by an oblong, rounded object: perhaps a baseball bat. This had occurred sometime during the middle hours of the morning after breakfast. Ed had apparently been the only one on the third floor, except of course for the person who had bashed in his head.

Frank Dillon stood looking at what had been Ed Walch lying there twisted on the second-floor stair landing and shook his head.

"What in the hell is going on here?" he exclaimed barely under his breath.

Michelle Neubrander stared at the body as if uncomprehending, and although she heard Frank's exclamation, she didn't respond.

"I want everyone in the drawing room now!" Frank bellowed. "God damn, we're going to get to the bottom of this!"

It took some time to assemble everyone in the drawing room. Only Vincent Lowler and Marjorie Cosgrove were still in the house, in addition of course to Edna Wahl, Francie Benniger, and Juan Ortiz who was outside attending to his gardening duties. Elizabeth and Jason Ryder had gone to a gym to work out, Marvin Cosgrove had driven to an auto parts store, and Andy Walch was simply not there. No one knew where he had gone or when he would be back. Frank decided to begin interviewing everyone without waiting for Andy to return.

Frank Dillon began the interviews with Vincent Lowler and Marjorie Cosgrove since they were immediately accessible. Vincent Lowler claimed no knowledge of Ed Walch's activities after breakfast and had assumed Ed had left the property with everyone else. He did not know that Marjorie Cosgrove had remained behind as well because she had a headache. He believed that he and the house staff were the only ones in the house after breakfast. He had cleared the dishes to the kitchen where Edna Wahl was cleaning up. Juan Ortiz was helping him clear the dishes from the dining room to subsequently clean them. Juan had completed that task and had gone outside to attend to his gardening work, specifically mowing the lawn. Vincent could verify Juan's outside activities because he could hear the lawnmower through his basement window. Vincent had stayed in his office/kitchen/living room after clearing the breakfast dishes and had done some financial paperwork; specifically, he had worked on the quarterly tax report for the bed-and-breakfast. He didn't realize there was anything wrong until he heard Francie Benniger, the housekeeper, scream. He did not kill Ed Walch and did not know who had or why they had.

Marjorie Cosgrove had gone to her room after breakfast complaining of a headache. She had complained of this headache to her husband and to Francie Benniger who had knocked on her room to change the towels and sheets. She wasn't really asleep when she was startled by Francie's scream. She ran out of her room on the second floor to see Francie standing over the prone body of Ed Walch, who lay at the bottom of the stairs from the third floor in a contorted position. Marjorie could tell immediately that he was dead because of the way his body was twisted; it was humanly impossible for a body to be in that position and be alive. At the very least, his back or neck would have been broken. She didn't know Ed Walch well and could think of no reason why anyone would want to kill him.

Francie Benniger had knocked on the Cosgroves' door and was told by Marjorie, through the closed door, that Marjorie had a headache and could Francie come back later. She had then gone across the hall to Izzy Dulles's vacant room to make sure the flowers she had put in the room yesterday were still fresh. It was then that she thought she heard a strange sound coming from the end of the hall by the stairs. It sounded like an exaggerated thumping noise. The door to Izzy's room was open, so she could hear the sounds fairly distinctly. She went out into the hall to see what had happened, and she saw Ed Walch lying at the foot of the stairs on the second floor landing, looking all distorted. As she rushed up to him, she could see a large amount of blood pooling under his head. That was when and why she screamed. She didn't know of any reason why anyone would want Ed Walch dead.

Edna Wahl was in the kitchen when she heard Francie scream. The kitchen is on the main floor and the door was open, so she heard the scream clearly. She rushed out of the kitchen and up the stairs as quickly as she could, for she was very stout, and saw Francie and Marjorie standing over Ed Walch with their hands covering their mouths and, in Francie's case, face. Prior to that, she had been in the kitchen the entire morning cooking breakfast, cleaning the kitchen after breakfast, and preparing to make lunch. Vincent had seen her there, as had Juan when he cleaned the dishes, and

Francie had stopped down for a glass of orange juice for a few minutes. Edna had no knowledge of why anyone would want to kill Ed Walch.

Juan Ortiz had helped Vincent clear the dining room and had washed the breakfast dishes in the sink in the kitchen. Edna had been there the entire time, and Francie had been there for a few minutes. After cleaning the dishes, he had gone out into the yard to mow the grass, which he continued to do until he was called in for questioning by Officer Neubrander. He had neither seen nor heard anything pertinent to the death of Ed Walch. He did not know why anyone would want to kill Ed Walch.

Marvin Cosgrove was the first of the boarders to return. Marjorie had complained to him of a headache after breakfast and, since she intended to lie down in their room, he decided to go to the auto parts store on Mountain City Highway to pick up a trash bag for their car. It was something that he reserved to do when Marjorie was otherwise occupied since she had no interest in those kinds of things. He had no knowledge of the incident at the house until he walked through the front door and was immediately ushered into the drawing room to be questioned. He had not even had a chance to see Marjorie, and was she all right? He had no idea why anyone would want to kill Ed Walch, and he had no idea where Andy Walch went.

The Ryders also knew nothing of the events at the bed-and-breakfast after leaving to go to the gym. They had gone to a gym off of Fifth Street on the other side of the I-80 Freeway and had walked the entire way there and back. It was a long walk, but refreshing. Both had felt that they needed some physical activity after the week's horrible events, and this seemed like the best alternative. Several people had seen them at the gym although they hadn't really spoken to anyone or learned their names, but they had registered when they entered. Although they both felt that Ed Walch was kind of obnoxious, they could not see why anyone would want to kill him.

Finally, Andy Walch returned to the house. When Frank Dillon told him about his cousin's demise, he slumped into one of the chairs in the drawing room with a red face and stared out of the window. His breathing became shallower, and Michelle had to get a paper bag for him to breathe into. Frank, concerned over Andy's reddening complexion and difficulty in breathing, called for medical attention. Upon their arrival, the paramedics administered oxygen to Andy through a mask and advised Frank that they were going to take Andy to the hospital for a checkup, just in case. Frank and Michelle followed the ambulance to the hospital and waited in the emergency area, watching the tests being done to Andy. The doctor finally nodded to Frank that he could speak to Andy, whose complexion at that point looked almost normal.

It turned out that Andy had not wanted anyone to know where he had gone, so he hadn't told anyone, including his cousin. He had walked to one of the bordellos on Third Street and had spent three hundred dollars to be with a prostitute named Tiffany. He was pretty certain that she would remember him; he didn't notice Michelle's raised eyebrow at this comment and her slight snicker directed most certainly to Frank, who did notice. After leaving Tiffany, he had walked down to Water Street and then over to the Fifth Street bridge, under which he had gone to cross the railroad tracks and to walk along the Humboldt River. He had thrown some rocks into the river and watched some ducks fly away and had then walked back to the bed-and-breakfast house. If only he had told Ed what he was going to do, perhaps Ed would have accompanied him and would still be alive! He didn't know why Ed was killed and couldn't imagine anyone having any reason to cause his cousin's demise. Ed was a wonderful man who had never hurt anyone.

At the conclusion of this interview, Frank and Michelle gave Andy a ride back to the bed-and-breakfast house on Silver Street. Frank directed everyone to congregate in the dining room, including the house staff, and then went into the drawing room to make a phone call. When he returned, he announced that all of the boarders were going to be moved to the Stockmen's Hotel, at the county's expense, for the rest of their stay in Elko. The staff of the house was free to go to their homes but was not to leave town, and the bed-and-breakfast was going to be closed down until Frank was able to get to the bottom of these terrible events. Amidst the protests, Frank stood resolute and answered the questions, or demands, from those quarantined and from Vincent Lowler who saw the ominous resultant decline in income.

"Look!" Frank practically shouted. "Until we know why these crimes were committed, we can't afford to let you stay here! We don't know if the crimes are related to this house, or if they are completely unrelated and specific to the decedents. You can't leave town until we know more, and I can't let you stay here! You are going to have to make the best of it! I promise you we are working as fast as we can to solve this, but until we know what is behind this, I doubt that you will be safer anywhere else in the country! For now, you are stuck in Elko! Now go pack your things. Some officers are on their way here to move you to the Stockmen's."

The opening of the front door revealed the arrival of three police cars to move the boarders and their belongings to the Stockmen's Hotel on Commercial Street. Frank preceded the procession and made the necessary reservations at the hotel. He made certain that all of the boarders were housed on one floor of the hotel, which unfortunately was the top floor. He arranged to post a guard on that floor to be present when any of the boarders were in attendance and informed the boarders that they were not to go anywhere alone or unattended.

When this was finished and the cacophonous protests had settled down, Frank sat down with Michelle in the restaurant of the hotel.

"Our asses are going to be in a sling if we don't get this worked out very soon!" he declared to Michelle as a waitress poured the coffee. "The county is not going to go for the kind of money we're putting out here without some pretty tangible results."

"But what are we going to do?" Michelle asked, the concern poignant in her voice. "We've looked at everything, and there is just nothing to go on!"

"Let's look at what we've got," Frank suggested. He put up his hand to ward off Michelle's intended protest. "I know we've gone over everything again and again. But let's do it again. The forensics has given us very little. There was no trace evidence of anyone outside those in the house, but that doesn't mean much. We have the knife that killed Benjamin, but it is a knife from the kitchen that anyone could have taken at anytime. We haven't found whatever was used to kill Ed, most probably a baseball bat. What else?"

Michelle shrugged. "Whoever killed Ed Walch was up on the third floor with him, but could have gone out the fire escape. No one admits to being up there, and no one was seen up there. Everyone seems to have an alibi of some sort, same as with Benjamin. I don't know, it seems like we're up against a wall here with no place else to go!"

Frank shook his head. "We're missing something. These are not just random crimes. Two murders have been committed in the same house within a week's time. What does that tell us?"

Michelle furrowed her brow in thought.

"Well," she began, "unless we believe in coincidence, the murders must have something to do with the house. To think that two completely unrelated murders can occur in the same house in a week's time boggles the imagination. The only other connection I can think of is the family. The victims are related."

"But is the perpetrator related to the victims?" Frank asked.

"I guess we won't know that until we find out who did it," Michelle commented, sipping her coffee.

Frank agreed. "For now, I think we have two lines of possibility that we need to concentrate on. One is the house, and the other is the family. The murders have to be related to one or the other. Even if the perpetrator is not related to the victims, the connection has to be either the house or the family. Either the murderer is trying to keep people from discovering something in the house, or perhaps that legend, or there is a grievance against the family."

"Sounds reasonable," Michelle reflected. "So what do we do now?"

Frank grinned mischievously. "Pick your poison," he said. "Which do you want to run to ground—the house or the family? You take one, and I'll take the other. That way, we'll get this done more quickly."

Michelle thought for a moment. "I guess I'll take the family," she answered uncertainly. "I can't see where to go with the house. I can't see why anyone would kill over that house. And if by 'the house' you mean the legend about the gold, that legend has been around for over a hundred years and nobody has found it yet. If you have to find the gold to find the killer, well, I just don't see me doing it. At least with the family, I can do some investigating, some research."

"Fair enough," Frank responded. "I'll take the house. And by 'the house,' I do mean the legend. I need to find out more about that legend. I think that means I need to go to the source."

"The source?" questioned Michelle.

"James Vanderlin himself," Frank said with a grin.

CHAPTER 22

Virginia City (1866)

James Vanderlin stood on the steps of the courthouse in Virginia City next to his new wife. He had just married Rebecca Wilkes in a civil proceeding conducted by the justice of the peace. He was not smiling, but Rebecca was. She was practically ebullient, in a flush of excitement, her face red with joy. James was squinting against the morning sunlight, trying to shield his eyes with his upstretched arm, his face contorted in a grimace.

It wasn't that James doubted his decision to marry again. James seldom second-guessed his decisions. They were generally made with a certain amount of consideration and forethought if time and circumstances permitted. This decision had been developing in different stages since James first came to Virginia City. After the incident with Lars Foley, it began to dawn on James that he would not be accepted into the society to which he aspired. He was considered an outsider, and one with a sullied reputation.

It astounded James how his deeds, no matter how hard he tried to conceal them, came back to haunt him. After killing Lars Foley, James secretly bought the mine claim, which had become Foley's final resting place, through an intermediary. Through another intermediary, he offered to buy Foley's mercantile store from Foley's widow. Although James, to those few that he disclosed his participation in this endeavor, claimed he wanted to purchase the store to help Foley's widow financially, he truthfully wanted another outlet for his leather goods to be sold. He thought that he could make a wise and frugal financial investment through buying the store from the woman who was facing financial difficulties as a result of her husband's disappearance. Additionally, it, along with the leather goods industry, presented a more legitimate picture than James's other enterprises.

Unfortunately, the details of who was actually buying the store ultimately leaked out, and the public outcry against James became uncomfortable. Many people in the city believed James responsible for the disappearance of Lars Foley since most knew of Foley's antipathy for James, and some actually knew of his plan for James. Nothing was proven, however, but the clamor resulted in people boycotting the store and the store ultimately going bankrupt.

During this time, James had the entrance to the mine which held Foley's body dynamited to prevent any possible discovery of the truth. The dynamiting of the mine entrance proved both providential and unfortunate for James. The dynamiting of the entrance, while ensuring that Foley's tomb would remain hidden, revealed another vein of gold that had been previously undiscovered, and it proved to be entirely within James's claim. However, the discovery of this gold ultimately revealed the true owner of the mine claim to be James. The resultant publicity over this ownership made the people of Virginia City even more suspicious of James and his secretive practices. James's need for respectability was moving further and further out of his reach.

Oddly enough, it was one of James's men—Angus McPhersen, who was known as Scotty because of his Scottish heritage and was one of the two men who had knifed the unfortunate Jacob Berentsen—who suggested the solution to James's dilemma.

"You need a wife," McPhersen commented to James's verbal complaint about being disrespected by the townspeople.

"What was that?" James queried, somewhat surprised by a comment from one of his men that sounded perceptive and considered.

McPhersen shrugged. "I think you need a wife, boss. Someone respectable. A lady. I mean a real lady. Someone the people of this town would look up to."

James contemplated. "Um," he said thoughtfully. "What would that do?"

McPhersen was taken aback that James would solicit his opinion on something he had thrown out on a whim. He was used to James dismissing his comments with a wave of his hand or simply ignoring them altogether. McPhersen was constantly confused by James's rhetorical questions and usually got caught in the trap of responding when no response was wanted. James, on the other hand, was given to thinking out loud and was startled when given a response to one of his abstract thoughts. He usually found it irritatingly distracting but not worth commenting on.

McPhersen straightened his normally slouched stance. "I knew a man once in San Antonio. He was a gambler and a cheat—I think. Anyway, this man met a woman who was highborn and somehow got her to marry him. From then on, this man took on airs, and everyone seemed to think he was something. I think it was the woman who did it—made him respectable, I mean."

James looked at Scotty McPhersen differently for the first time. He thought of Scotty, along with his other men, as minions: men simply put on the earth to do his bidding. Although uneducated and not sophisticated, Scotty had offered something that illustrated more profound thinking than James was used to in his accomplices. He began to redesign his impressions of Scotty. Scotty, however, found it uncomfortable to be the focus of James's unwavering gaze. It usually forebode ill tidings. He let his posture slump to its usual stature and tried to appear less apparent.

"Very interesting, Scotty," James commented and turned back to his ledgers. Scotty realized he had been dismissed and left the office at the back of the saloon on E Street.

From that moment on, James Vanderlin looked for a wife. This was not as easy a task as one would think. Although James was a wealthy man that would appeal to a variety of avaricious women, he needed another kind of mate. He wanted a woman who was born of distinction, or who could present herself in such a way but would not be influenced by James's dark nature. He wanted someone to believe in him in spite of himself. Yet he did not want a remake of Josie, for he did not intend to replace Josie in his heart. In James's mind and in his heart, there could never again be another Josie. Josie had been respectable but had delighted in James. She had been the ideal woman, the goddess at the foot of whom James would always worship. Josie had seen James's dark nature but had not hidden from it; indeed, she had gloried in it. She had basked in the idea that her husband would never be anyone's minion but hers. She knew James would never betray her, would never let anyone harm her, would steal for her, and would die for her. The fact that she had died first was an accident of nature that would never find satisfaction or absolution in James's conscience.

James did not travel the globe looking for a suitable woman. He put these ideas to the back of his mind but paid attention to the gentler sex about him. He continued to ply his trades, to build his wealth, and to plow his road through the business of running those lives that he could touch around him. But he was aware now. He looked at each woman that came into his world with a critical eye, a discerning gaze of discrimination.

He became more aware of the effect he had on women, certain women, or perhaps it was the effect of his acknowledged wealth on these women. He studied the mannerisms of women and the men who were obviously attractive to women and practiced being around them. It reminded him of the time when he wanted Josie and stalked her and of the feeling that he would do anything to win her.

It was in this vein that he met Rebecca Wilkes. He was in San Francisco to attend to his saloon there in the Barbary Coast district and attended a formal dinner for one of the men running for office in that district. James was invited not because he was considered part of that circle but because he had money that could be purposed. Indeed, it was a surprise to the political solicitors when James actually appeared at the dinner as he had been solicited many times in the past and had never attended any similar function. The dinner was held at a private residence on Nobb Hill, the home of a state senator, and was lavishly appointed. James marveled at the luxury of the place and considered that perhaps there was money to be made in politics, an idea to which he had never given much thought.

The dinner table was a monstrous thing of almost fifty feet in length and seated perhaps fifty people. By chance, James was seated next to Rebecca. She was not young, approaching forty he thought. Yet she was attractive and had a dignity of bearing that impressed James. Rebecca Wilkes, it turned out, was the widow of the son of an industrialist who owned factories in Massachusetts. She herself had a son who was at that time a teenager and was the spitting image of his grandfather, although it profited her none. The grandfather had disowned his son, Rebecca, and his grandson when the three of them moved west to begin their own business. It turned out that the acorn did not fall near the tree when it came to business acumen, and Rebecca's husband soon was floundering in financial mire. He was a great disappointment to Rebecca as well as her son and his grandfather and chose to die a pauper in a riding accident, leaving his wife and son to rest upon the largess of good friends.

And so James Vanderlin and Rebecca Wilkes became acquainted. He thought her sophisticated and urbane and she thought him wild and rugged, and both very shortly decided that they would marry the other. James received the woman of respectability and substance who would come to love him in spite of his faults, and Rebecca found a man of wealth and ambition who could overcome all obstacles on their way to financial security and affluence. The match was encouraged by Rebecca's friends, who ignored the rumors of James's past and saw a reprieve from the financial burden of caring for Rebecca and her morose son.

Thus, on that sunny morning in Virginia City in the spring of 1866, James was not upset over having married Rebecca Wilkes. He was angry that few people—actually, none—had come to acknowledge the wedding. He had insisted on being married in Virginia City to cement that proclamation in the minds of the citizens there and, at the very least, expected someone from the *Territorial Enterprise* newspaper to be present. If Samuel Clemens had still been there, he at least would have offered some kind of comment, however unkind. But alas, Clemens, who had been such an irritant to James during the two years that Clemens had worked for the *Territorial Enterprise*, left the city for points further west almost two years ago. The rumor was that Clemens left Virginia City because of James's veiled threats and fear that something similar to what happened to Lars Foley would happen to him. James would never admit to any responsibility in the departure of Samuel Clemens from Virginia City but was, until this moment, glad of his leaving.

"Is something wrong, James?" Rebecca asked, suddenly concerned by James's contrary appearance.

"No, my dear," James countered, aware that Scotty's prediction of respectability might not be so easily achieved but needing to keep his thoughts on the subject private. "Let's go on up to the house."

The house was a three-story structure on Summit Street as high up the mountain as the town limits would permit, which James had built shortly after being taken from his hotel room during the Foley incident. James realized that he needed a sanctuary that was less accessible to the public and could be defended more properly. The top floor of the house was gabled and contained one large room and three smaller rooms. The large room was used primarily for storage, with the smaller rooms serving as maids' quarters. The second floor consisted of bedrooms, including the master bedroom that overlooked the town, and a privy. The first floor contained the living room, drawing room, dining room, music room, kitchen, and another privy, which the servants and day guests used. The first floor connected to the second floor via a magnificent staircase along the side wall of the living room, with hand-carved mahogany rails and a plush carpet runner made in the orient. The second-floor balcony overlooked the living room and allowed access to the bedrooms. At the end of the hallway from the balcony was a simple staircase that led to the third floor.

Rebecca had seen the house only once prior to her wedding day but was delighted with its accommodations. In her mind she was already redesigning the interiors to reflect a more feminine and sophisticated approach. James tended toward dark woods and sparse furnishings, although of high quality. Rebecca envisioned a more aristocratic residence with lots of lace and velvet and impressive paintings adorning the walls. She had already decided on a back bedroom away from the master bedroom for her son Eli who was sixteen years old and motivated by sullen and self-involved thoughts. Eli was to join Rebecca and James in Virginia City in a week's time, her friends in San Francisco having agreed to keep him that much longer to give Rebecca and James time to adjust to each other.

As James and Rebecca and Scotty, who had officially witnessed the marriage, walked up to the house on Summit Street, James reflected in his mind on his hope for a new beginning for his future, perhaps a future that involved politics.

CHAPTER 23

Virginia City (Present Day)

Frank Dillon entered The Way it Was Museum on C Street in Virginia City. He had already been to the visitor's center, the Gambler's Museum, the Territorial Enterprise Museum, and the Julia Bulette Red Light Museum. He was trying to learn as much as he could about James Vanderlin and was being frustrated at every turn. It seemed that James Vanderlin was a historical ghost when it came to information of a personal nature. Very little was documented regarding his time in Virginia City, or elsewhere for that matter. It was as if Vanderlin had made a conscious effort to be anonymous.

There were several archived newspaper articles at the Territorial Enterprise Museum that mentioned Vanderlin, rarely in a complimentary fashion, and one that described his wife Rebecca as a social mistress. Apparently, her parties were not well attended. There was a notice indicating that James Vanderlin had lost an election to another resident of Virginia City to sit on the city council. There were also obituaries for both Rebecca and James Vanderlin. It was noted that Rebecca Wilkes Vanderlin died of pneumonia in 1872, survived by her husband and her son Eli Wilkes. James Vanderlin died in the great fire of 1875 when a good part of Virginia City was consumed in flames. The cause of the fire was claimed to be a coal oil lamp that had been knocked over in one of the boardinghouses, but that claim has never been confirmed.

At the Julia Bulette Red Light Museum, Frank learned that there might be pictures of James Vanderlin's first wife and daughter in The Way it Was Museum. Although the famous prostitute Julia Bulette had died of strangulation due to homicide in 1867, another prostitute of Julia's acquaintance had nursed Rebecca Wilkes during her tragic illness and had been told of the pictures by Rebecca between her deliriums. Rebecca Vanderlin had reviled these pictures for their reverence from her husband. This prostitute, Alice Merchant, had been enthralled by the sadness of Rebecca's story and had secretly rescued the paintings after James Vanderlin's death when Vanderlin's possessions were being systematically looted. The paintings had survived to the present day and were ensconced in the attic of The Way it Was Museum.

Frank's identification as a police officer got him access to the attic of The Way it Was Museum where old, odd furnishings and antique clothing were stored in a helter-skelter manner. The elderly lady from the front desk of the museum pointed Frank in the general direction where she thought the paintings were in the attic and muttered that she could not stay with him as she was the only employee working at that time. It did not take long for Frank to find the two paintings in question. There were other pictures and paintings scattered about, but the two of interest were the only ones of women of that period. The paintings showed two individual women that appeared related in that they wore similar fashions and had similar facial and body characteristics. They were attractive women, but it was difficult to distinguish their ages. Both women seemed to be of similar ages, and Frank could not tell which was mother and which was daughter.

He took the paintings downstairs to the front-desk lady and asked if she could distinguish the individuals in them. The lady could not. Then, much to the elderly lady's consternation, Frank wrote a receipt for the paintings and left with them under his arm before anyone could stop him. He fully expected to receive a visit at his room in the Gold Hill Hotel from the Storey County sheriff—a visit which never materialized. Little did Frank know that the elderly lady never mentioned his caper to anyone, and the museum staff was astounded some months later when they received a crate from Frank containing those very same paintings. The museum staff hadn't known that the paintings were missing.

Back at his room in the Gold Hill Hotel, Frank phoned Michelle Neubrander on her cell phone and left a message for her to call him. He then called his sergeant at the Elko Police Department to report in and to describe his activities. Michelle called back within the hour.

"Where are you?" Frank asked.

"I'm in Springfield, Illinois," Michelle answered. "I have just finished talking to the Ryder siblings' grandmother."

"And?" Frank encouraged after waiting some moments for Michelle to go on.

"Nothing out of the ordinary," Michelle continued. "They pretty much check out. Their dad died a couple of months ago. Their mom left years ago with no after contact. They don't have any other relatives in the area, and the grandmother says they never had any contact from the others in this mess until just recently. It seems they had never met any of their relatives until this last week. How about you?"

Frank reiterated what he had discovered, which seemed fairly paltry.

"What are you going to do next?" Michelle inquired.

Frank shook his head as if Michelle could see him. "Don't know for sure. One of the people in one of the museums here mentioned that he thought the Eli Wilkes family came from the east somewhere. He thought Massachusetts and that they were involved in some kind of manufacturing during the last century or so. I thought I might check it out."

"Are you going to go there?" Michelle asked.

"Not right away," Frank responded. "I need to find out more. I'll send teletypes from the office and look on the Internet before I do anything."

"I think I'll do the same." Frustration tinged Michelle's voice. "This was a lot of nothing. A long trip for not much return."

Michelle clearly did not enjoy the travel aspect of their present assignment. She enjoyed the comfort of her home, and living out of a suitcase in a place she would not have chosen to visit under any other circumstance was not to her liking, especially if she had to do it alone. If Margo had come with her, she might have liked visiting the tomb of Abraham Lincoln or the Illinois State Capitol building. But as it was, she was simply anxious to leave.

After hanging up the phone with Michelle, Frank sat for a time studying the paintings of the Vanderlin women. There was something oddly familiar about the paintings, but he couldn't put his finger on what it was. There was certainly nothing particularly unique about the pictures. If one put the paintings side by side, it seemed as if the women were facing toward each other as much as toward the painter. Their poses were similar and obviously staged. The faces of the women, with slight differences, were also similar to the point that it almost seemed as if it were the same woman in different poses. Yet the color of the hair was slightly different, and one woman seemed somewhat smaller than the other. Frank suspected the smaller woman was probably the daughter, but that may have been simply his prejudice.

Frank decided to drive back up the hill to Virginia City from Gold Hill and eat dinner at the Bucket of Blood Saloon. He had a taste for a large juicy cheeseburger with lots of onions and pickles, the kind of thing he couldn't eat at home without his wife giving him one of her looks. "The look" was worse than a verbal criticism, for he couldn't respond to "the look" verbally, or she would simply shake her head in disgust without saying a word, as if no word was needed or worthy, and walk away. It always left him feeling incomplete, like he was caught doing something that inaccurately appeared reprehensible but he wasn't given the chance to explain. The burger was everything that he imagined on his drive up the mountain, and when he was finished eating, he felt happily bloated. The french fries and the beer chaser completed the whole package to his entire satisfaction.

Back at the Gold Hill Hotel, Frank got into bed, set the timer on the television to turn off in an hour, and went to sleep. The sun had not yet set, but that didn't bother Frank at all. At eleven that evening, when Frank was deep into his sleep, his cell phone rang. It took Frank several moments to realize what the noise meant, and he automatically glanced at his watch as he answered the call.

"Frank?" came the voice on the phone. The voice sounded familiar.

"What?" the word stumbled out of Frank's mouth. "Who is this?"

"It's Lieutenant Brubaker, Frank," the voice declared. Lieutenant Brubaker was his sergeant's boss. "There's been a problem."

Frank sat up in the bed, the sleep quickly clearing from his mind. This couldn't be good, Frank thought. Something must have happened.

"What's going on?" he asked.

"The Cosgroves are dead!" the lieutenant answered. "That husband-and-wife couple at the Stockmen's—they've been murdered, we think."

Frank let this sink into his brain. "What do you mean they've been murdered?"

"Don't know yet. They're dead, lying on their bed. No signs of violence. The coroner thinks they've been poisoned. We won't know for sure until we get the results back. You better get back here!"

CHAPTER 24

Virginia City (January 1872)

James Vanderlin stormed out of the bedroom on the second floor of his house on Summit Street. The bedroom had been converted into an office, and in the office was a large rolltop desk made of teak wood that James kept locked. He had the only key to the desk lock, yet the watch that Josie had given him was missing from the drawer where it was normally kept.

"Where's my watch!" he screamed down the hall, and leaning on the rail overlooking the downstairs living room, he screamed it again.

The maid downstairs went scurrying out of view, terrified. James did not wait for an answer but hurtled down the stairs in time to see Rebecca emerge from the music room.

"Where's my watch!" he shouted again, this time glowering at Rebecca who cowered against the wall next to the music room.

"I-I haven't seen it!" she stammered.

"I'll bet your son has!" James continued threateningly, unrelenting. "Where is he?"

"He's not here," Rebecca responded, fear tingeing her voice. "He's gone out. He won't be back for a while. But he couldn't have taken it! He wouldn't have! You're the only one with a key to that desk!"

"Ah, so you know where I keep it, do you?" James grabbed Rebecca by the shoulders, shaking her violently. She closed her eyes and turned her head away from his rage. James thrust her back against the wall, down which she slid and came to rest on the floor, sobbing. James turned and stalked away.

James walked down the street to his saloon on E Street and marched into his office at the back of the saloon, slamming the door. This was not an unusual occurrence in the last couple of years, except that it was becoming more frequent. The employees of the saloon had become used to James's rages and knew to stay out of his way. He was not averse to beating someone before firing them if they didn't anticipate his required need for space and solitude.

Things had not gone as James had wished or anticipated. Marrying Rebecca had not been the miracle cure to redeeming his reputation. It wasn't that Rebecca hadn't tried to be that kind of spouse to James; she had given party after party, from garden parties to formal dinners. Yet few townspeople attended. At first, her friends would journey from San Francisco at her pleading, but as time went on, even they stopped coming. Instead of her redeeming James's reputation, it seemed that he sullied hers. It was as if the darkness in James was a fire lit in a peat bog that would never go out and, little by little, spread to all around.

James missed Josie. She and only she had had the ability to walk through James's darkness with what seemed like a warm light, inviting those around to the comfort of coziness. She would have made this work. She would have taken James's hard edges, his verging on barbarity, and made them soft to the outside world. She would have made sense of his needs and reached effortlessly to their fulfillment. She and Jessie had filled that gaping hole of desperate emptiness inside James that pushed him to the edge of atrocity. Without her, that hole became a cauldron of rage that unceasingly boiled, often spilling over its edges to some calamity.

No amount of ill-gained wealth seemed to alleviate the loneliness inside James or his resultant desire to hurt those around him. After all these years, he still could not accept being cheated out of his happiness with Josie and had to blame someone—anyone—for his abject loneliness. It was as if his real purpose had died with Josie and could never be revived. As much as he sought it, there was no Jesus standing at his corner resurrecting his beloved Lazarus. James sat at his desk, his head in his hands, and seethed and cried. It was too much for any man to endure, and finally, James reached for the bottle of whiskey that sat at the edge of the desk and began pouring his salvation.

Unfortunately, salvation did not come in the form of forgetfulness. The alcohol reminded him that he was having more and more difficulty remembering the faces of his beloved wife and daughter, and even looking at their pictures more and more often could no longer cement them into his mind. In this stupor, James did not consider Rebecca his wife. She was an interloper who aspired to the throne of his heart, but she was not worthy. She and her worthless son, who was now twenty-two and utterly useless, were of no value to James. She had not fulfilled her promise in his mind, which was to give him the respectability that he deserved. She was not his wife! Josie was and always would be his wife, his only wife!

With these angry thoughts occupying his mind, James stumbled out of the saloon and made his way up the hill to his house. It had turned blisteringly cold, and a blizzard was just beginning in the growing darkness. James homed in on the warm lights emanating from his large house. Too many lights—a waste of gas, a waste! James could not consider that it may have been these many lights that kept him on his path to the house, for the blowing snow had practically taken away all visibility.

When he reached the house, James trod shakily up to the office/bedroom, unlocked his desk, and again looked for his watch. Although it was not in the drawer where it was supposed to be, he found the watch in the drawer next to it. Had he put it in the wrong drawer all along, he wondered? No! It was impossible! He had that watch in and out of the same drawer all of the time! He wouldn't have made that mistake. Someone must have been in his desk! How else could he account for this disgrace?

He went looking for Eli, Rebecca's twenty-two-year-old son. Eli was not in his room, and Rebecca was not in her room. James trekked downstairs, looking for either one to engage in a confrontation. He found Rebecca in the music room, sitting in a high-backed chair reading under a candlelit floor lamp. She stood when James thrust open the door, letting her book fall to the floor.

"Where is he?" James bellowed.

"He left when he found out what kind of mood you were in," Rebecca stated, standing her ground. James crossed the room and slapped her hard across the face, knocking her to the floor. He reached down and grabbed her roughly by the arm, lifting her to her feet and up off her feet.

"I want him out of this house!" he raged inches from her face, which was beginning to glow red from the hideous slap. "I know he's the one who's been in my desk, sneaking around this house like a common thief! I know you wouldn't dare! You don't have the balls!"

James thrust her away from him, throwing her back to the floor in a pile of flounced material. Rebecca's head hit the edge of the side table causing a gash in her scalp, which immediately began to bleed.

"I'll find him and tear his heart out!" James continued in his wrath.

Rebecca sat up against the table, ignoring the blood streaming down her face.

"You will not!" she screamed. "If you do anything, I will have you arrested! How will that look on your precious reputation?" she said this with vehemence dripping with sarcasm.

James grabbed her by her hair and again lifted her up. This time, however, he dragged her across the room, out the door, down the hall, and thrust her out the front door and down the steps into the blowing snow.

"You can get out with him!" he bellowed, closing and locking the door.

Rebecca struggled to her feet, climbed the steps, and tried to enter the house. The door was securely bolted and would not budge to her tearful urges. She banged on the door, crying for help from the household staff. No one came to help her. The house staff had hurried to their rooms and had hidden themselves away, not daring to counter the master of the house. Rebecca slumped to the deck of the porch sobbing, holding herself in a fetal position. She lay there for hours before Eli finally came home and found her thus. Incredulous, he bundled her up in his coat and struggled with her down to the nearest boardinghouse, one block down the hill and a block over.

Rebecca never again entered the house on Summit Street. She lingered in the boardinghouse for a week until she died of the pneumonia she had contracted that night. During that week, she was cared for by Alice Merchant, a twenty-two-year-old Boston girl who had come to Virginia City not more than a month previous with her father who had almost immediately been killed in a mine accident. Alice was left to fend for herself and had turned to prostitution to sustain her life in that hard clime. She saw the pity in Rebecca's circumstances and nurtured her as best she could, but there was little she could do but make Rebecca's last days as comfortable as possible.

Rebecca, for her part, saw Alice as her son's contemporary and trusted Alice with her deliriums, dreaming of a happy life for Eli and Alice as partners in life. This, of course, was never to be, for Eli was to follow a different path and Alice was pariah to polite society. The fantasy of the dream, however, gave Rebecca some joy in her last gasps of life.

CHAPTER 25

Stockmen's Hotel (Present Day)

Marvin and Marjorie Cosgrove lay upon their bed as if they were peacefully asleep. While the medical examiner and the forensics team had already done their work, they had left the bodies until Frank Dillon could view them in their state of demise. Frank observed the bodies with the disdain and frustration of having failed to prevent a catastrophe whose cause was a complete mystery to him. It was as if a plague of death had descended upon Elko. With Frank's approval, Marvin and Marjorie were removed to the morgue for autopsy.

Instead of driving from Virginia City to Elko, which would have taken five hours, Frank drove to the nearest airport in Carson City where the Nevada Department of Public Safety's plane was waiting for him. The plane, on loan to the Elko Police Department for this trip, flew Frank directly to Elko in less than two hours. Frank would have to arrange for his department vehicle to be brought back from the airport in Carson City. He would again check with the Department of Public Safety, for with their varied divisions—including the Nevada Highway Patrol, the Division of Parole and Probation, and the Nevada Division of Investigation—someone would likely be making the journey to Elko.

If the Cosgroves had been poisoned, the instrument of their deaths could be anything. Only they could tell what they had eaten and when, and they weren't talking. Frank hoped that the autopsy would reveal something, but they had most probably ingested whatever killed them before they went to bed the previous evening. The maid had opened the door to their room at eleven in the morning of the next day to change the sheets and towels and had seen them sleeping so had not entered the room. Their deaths hadn't been discovered until seven that evening when the police officer guarding that floor became suspicious of the Cosgroves' inactivity. That was almost a full twenty-four hours between their likely deaths and their discovery. Frank wondered what evidence would be left in their stomachs.

Interviews with the maid and all of the other hotel maids, as well as the maintenance supervisor, revealed that the principal maid was the only person admitting to going into the Cosgroves' room during that two-day period. Then again, it was possible that no one in the hotel was responsible for putting the poison in front of the Cosgroves, that someone could have put poison in the Cosgroves' meal at the Star Restaurant on Third Street where they were observed to eat their supper. Consequently, the staff of the Star Restaurant was interviewed, with no "smoking gun" being revealed.

Previously, the suspects/potential victims/bed-and-breakfast boarders were only guarded on the top floor of the Stockmen's Hotel at night. Since the previous murders had occurred at the bed-and-breakfast on Silver Street and the Elko Police Department's resources were limited, Frank had not tried to prescribe the participants' movements apart from the hotel. He had only admonished the boarders to let the police department know where they were going and when.

The guard on the top floor of the hotel was not a complete protection detail but was principally in place overnight when the potential victims were sleeping. His shift usually started at ten o'clock in the evening and lasted until eight the next morning.

With the Cosgrove murders, it became clear to Frank that this limited protection was not going to be enough. Since the Elko Police Department's resources had not improved since Frank's last decision, Frank declared that the remaining boarders, now down to the Ryder siblings and Andy Walch, were not to go anywhere without each other and without a police escort. This required an around-the-clock shift of police officers, one each shift, to complete the task of protecting the survivors. This would increase the protection detail by two officers, not an unreasonable addition of expense to the department. It was very restrictive to the survivors but was received without complaint by the Ryders and Andy Walch, for they were obviously frightened. Either there was a serial murderer in the vicinity targeting very specific victims or one of them was that murderer. It was in all their interests to keep together under the watchful eye of a police officer.

After this was done, Frank headed home to get some sleep. He had had less than two hours' sleep the night before and was exhausted. Just as Frank was climbing into bed that early afternoon, Michelle Neubrander arrived at the Elko airport from Illinois. She was well rested and hadn't heard a word about the goings-on in Elko until her arrival at the department. She was understandably amazed. This was her first homicide case, and it was turning into a blizzard of killings. While waiting for Frank to finish his rest, she decided to go on with her research into the Vanderlin descendants, this time utilizing the Internet and the telephone.

Frank arrived back at the station at four that afternoon. He was not completely rested, for his afternoon nap was restless, but at least he could think properly. Frank's meeting with Michelle was not joyful. They fully briefed each other on what they had found on their trips away from Elko.

"What are we gonna do?" Michelle asked with some trepidation.

"We have to go on with our plan," Frank declared. "It's the only plan we have, and we can't be distracted by events. Unless you can think of something better to do?"

Michelle shook her head.

"I want you to expand your search of family to include the staff at the bed-and-breakfast," Frank directed. "Even though they have been here in Elko for years with no apparent problem, we can't eliminate them as suspects. Of the boarders, there's only three left. So either one of them is a murderer, or it's one of the staff of the bed-and-breakfast."

"What about the staff of the Stockmen's?" Michelle asked. "The last murders occurred there."

Frank pondered this for a moment. "I don't think so," he said finally. "The murders started before we moved them to the Stockmen's, and nobody there knew we were going to move the boarders to that hotel. It would be a huge leap for someone there to have anticipated all of this."

Michelle nodded. The logic of Frank's argument made sense to her.

Frank turned to leave but stopped in midstep and added, "Just to be sure, check with the Stockmen's and find out if they hired anyone after we moved everyone."

Again, Michelle nodded. "What are you going to do?" she asked.

"I'm going to the morgue to sit in on the autopsy," he replied, putting on his jacket.

The autopsy on Marvin Cosgrove was already completed, and the one on Marjorie was almost done by the time Frank arrived at the morgue.

"Find anything?" Frank asked.

The medical examiner shook his head. "I've sent samples to tox to see what is in the blood and the organs. There were no signs of violence, so it will have to be in the tox. All of the indicators read arsenic poisoning, however. You can see it in the fingernails and in the lips. By the way, the forensics team found chocolate wrappers in the wastebasket, so it's possible that's how it was administered. Someone could have tampered with those little chocolates they put on the pillows."

Frank nodded, pleased. "Well that's something anyway."

Frank called Michelle to tell her what he had learned from the medical examiner.

"Do you think it is arsenic poisoning?" Michelle asked. "Do you think that's what they'll find?"

"I'm sure of it," Frank responded.

"By the way," Michelle interjected into a long pause, "there were four people hired at the Stockmen's during the last two weeks: a craps dealer, two maids, and a maintenance worker. Three were hired since we moved the boarders there—the two maids and the maintenance worker."

"I see," Frank responded. "See what you can find out about them. Where they came from, why they came here—that sort of thing. I want you to interview them yourself. Don't give it to someone else. I want to make sure we get what we need out of them. We're running out of time on this thing!"

Frank said this despairingly. Michelle listened to him with concern. He sounded wounded and tired.

"Is this what it's like, Frank?" she asked. "Is this what working homicide is like?"

Frank laughed over the phone, a chilling laugh.

"No," he responded. "This isn't what it is like. Normally, it is cut and dried. A husband beats his wife to death, a wife stabs her husband. That's what you mostly deal with. Domestic stuff. Homicides are usually easy to figure out—the reasons are right in front of you. But they're no less tragic." He paused, reflecting. "This is different. This is like looking for gold. You know it's there, but you don't know where to look. You can be digging in one spot, and it can literally be a shovel width away and you would never know it. Sometimes it's just luck that you find the truth."

"Then how do we know what we're doing is the right thing?" Michelle asked.

"We don't," Frank said. "But you got to work a plan. Again, it's like looking for gold. You lay out a grid and you dig. You do it systematically, and if there's gold there, you have a better chance of finding it."

"I see," she said, and she really did. "So where do we go from here?"

"You continue with the family, and I work the treasure angle," Frank directed with determination and diligence. "You do the same with the staff at the bed-and-breakfast and with those four hired recently at the Stockmen's. I'm going to go home and get some sleep, and tomorrow I'm going to Boston."

"Boston?" Michelle inquired.

"Yah. I managed to find a living relative of Eli Wilkes on the Internet. He's out of the country on business, but his wife is there and she said she would see me, let me look through some family stuff—that kind of thing. Who knows, maybe we'll get lucky."

CHAPTER 26

Virginia City (1872)

Eli Wilkes stood above his stepfather James Vanderlin who lay sprawled across the fainting couch in the living room of the house on Summit Street. James was unconscious from drinking bourbon, the empty bottle lying tipped over on the rug next to the couch and inches from James's limp fingers. Eli looked down upon his stepfather with hatred, his face red with rage, his hands convulsively curling into fists. Yet Eli knew he would not hit James with his fists, for he was terrified of James and believed James would kill him when he awakened. It would be so easy to kill James, Eli thought, but he would not do so, for he did not know how and he didn't really believe that he could. Somehow James would survive, and then he would kill Eli. And this Eli believed with all of his heart.

Eli wasn't certain why he had come back to the house. Perhaps it was to see for one last time the home in which his mother had once been happy. His mother's happiness had not lasted long; of that Eli was certain. Yet he knew she had loved

James Vanderlin for, in spite of the way he treated her, she always defended him to Eli. His mother had died a week ago and Eli had been in hiding, for he believed his stepfather would kill him on sight. This was the degree of animosity between Eli and his stepfather. Eli had tried at the beginning to gain James's approval, but it had never happened. Eli was not ambitious or imaginative or particularly inclined toward hard labor, which was about the only occupation available to him. He did not possess the qualities that would have compelled James to look at him as worthy of note. He was not ruthless or cunning or possessing any particular intellect. In fact, he was not even as the average man on the Comstock, for he was averse to the backbreaking work ethic that possessed most of the men of their acquaintance.

Indeed, James's disapproval was displayed from the very beginning. It was probably the greatest reason for disagreement between his mother and James and perhaps the source of their eventual dysfunction and marital destruction. Eli felt this but could do nothing about it. He felt James's disrespect for him and saw James's progressive disrespect of his mother as time went on. Eli's failed attempts to become someone worthy made him more and more sullen and more and more angry. Yet his anger did not express outward, which probably would have gained James's attention and perhaps approval, but instead turned inward, making Eli more miserable. He lived inside himself and made himself scarce to the house whenever he could. He found hiding places in the abandoned mines around the town where he could play in his imagination the games of triumph and glory. This, of course, did not content James Vanderlin who saw his stepson as a ne'er-do-well and unworthy of continued support.

As long as Rebecca was alive, James could do nothing but financially support his stepson. That ended immediately with Rebecca's death. Eli had managed since his mother's death to live in the abandoned mines and to scavenge for food, but that could not last. He was desperate and needed to leave this place.

And so he stood in the house that he detested, looking down upon the man who had caused his life to become so wretched. It was not difficult for Eli to enter James's domain. Although the house was locked, he had practiced removing a glass pane from one of the side-door windows in the mudroom off to the side of the house, allowing him access whenever he pleased. This was usually when James was not at home, but on this occasion, he could not avoid the intrusion. He was determined to leave town, and he needed to see the place one last time. Also, he needed money.

This last thing is what inspired Eli to go into James's office and to open James's locked rolltop desk. He did this with a key that he removed from the drunken James's vest pocket. Not that he needed the key. He had previously broken into James's desk when he discovered one of the wood panels at the back of the desk was loose and could be pried open enough for him to reach in and release the lock. Using this method, he had actually removed James's precious pocket watch the week before his mother died and had walked around town with the watch tucked snugly in his pocket, feeling somehow superior to James. He had returned it that afternoon when he found what a commotion it had caused. For some reason, Eli did not relate that incident to his mother's eventual demise, which was probably a blessing.

Eli took the key to the desk from James's pocket because he was leaving and there was no longer any need for subterfuge. Additionally, he felt empowered by removing something so vital to James from James's very pocket. In that same vein, when he was taking gold coin freshly minted at the Carson City mint from the desk, he also removed his stepfather's pocket watch and put it in his pocket. This was not done from any conscious intent other than the fact that the watch was extremely important to James, and Eli imagined the pain that it would cause James when he realized that the watch was missing. He would like to have taken more money, but the huge floor safe in the corner was locked and Eli had never learned the combination. He would have to settle for the hundred or so dollars in gold coin found in the desk.

Eli left the house, leaving the front door wide open. The winter was beginning to turn, but there was still a cold wind blowing, which whistled through the house. It would eventually awaken the servants reposing on the top floor but likely not Vanderlin who was too drunk to care or to become conscious in the next few hours. That would give Eli some time to escape the town. Eli hoped the open door would be an invitation to others of a mercenary nature who might be prowling the cold night looking for shelter or plunder. He could imagine nothing more fitting than the demise of James Vanderlin at the hands of those with less compassion than Vanderlin himself. However unlikely this fantasy was, it made Eli smile as he walked to the stable.

Eli saddled one of the Vanderlin horses. He had intended to ride the horse to the Virginia and Truckee Railroad station at the edge of town and leave the horse there so that it wouldn't be considered horse theft, but when he got there he decided to pay the fee for the horse to be carried in the baggage car. Although he didn't want to hang for being a horse thief, and he had no doubt that Vanderlin would try to accuse him of that, he was Vanderlin's stepson and so felt that he could get away with the theft. Keeping the horse was an inspiration that would prove vital to Eli in the next hours.

The Virginia and Truckee Railroad train left at five that morning, making its way down the mountain through Gold Hill, crossing the Crown Point trestle above the hoists of the Yellow Jacket Mine, then through Mound House and Eureka to Carson City. At the Carson City depot, a gothic revival building on north Carson Street between Washington and Caroline Streets built that very year, Eli had to switch trains to go north through the Washoe Valley to Reno where he could catch the Central Pacific Railroad train to the East Coast. He intended to go to Boston where he hoped his grandfather would forgive his family's past transgressions and accept Eli into his bosom and charity. He didn't know if this was possible since he had never communicated with his grandfather. He was never particularly interested in that gentleman until now, but what choice did he have? He had never mastered any trade, nor did he have the desire to do so. Eli hoped his grandfather would forgive this deficiency and accept him as he was, by then probably penniless.

Eli had about a thirty-mile journey through the Washoe Valley to where he could connect to the Central Pacific Railroad that would take him east. He worried the entire journey, for it was now daylight and he didn't know how long James Vanderlin would remain unconscious. If James or one of his henchmen rode by horse straight north from Virginia City, they could arrive in Reno before Eli, although the trek down Mount Davidson was treacherous on horseback. Still, a good horseman could accomplish it without much ado. Perhaps Eli shouldn't have left the front door open. That would assure that the servants would awaken early, and if they discovered the office door and desk open, they might try to awaken Vanderlin before his natural course. That would be bad for Eli. Eli himself could have ridden the horse he had taken directly to Reno, but he didn't relish riding in the dark and the cold.

And so it came to be that when Eli arrived in Reno, departed the Virginia and Truckee Railroad, and maneuvered his horse to the back of a side building from the Central Pacific Railroad depot, he saw Angus McPhersen leaning against the wall of the ticket booth rolling a cigarette. McPhersen hadn't seen him. Eli hunched down against the side of the side building and cursed himself and his penchant for immature bravado. If only he hadn't left the front door open! What could he do now? He hadn't made an alternative plan!

Eli slowly realized that he would have to ride the horse he had stolen from Vanderlin to the next train station east—which would be Wadsworth, he remembered—and was probably twenty or thirty miles distant. But how often did the trains run? He couldn't even risk going into the depot to get a schedule. Again, he cursed his luck. Eli knew nothing about long-distance riding. He didn't know how to hunt or fish or trap game. He didn't even have a gun! He didn't have any blankets or clothing suitable for outdoor living. Eli began to openly sob in his frustration. Tears rolled down his face and onto the lapel of his over jacket.

A man walked by just then and saw the spectacle of Eli's torment. He wondered aloud after what catastrophe could cause a grown man to cry in public, and upon hearing of Eli's supply dilemma, took Eli in hand. The man knew of a wagon of pioneers who were discouraged and forsaken of their dream and were traveling back to the east. They would be glad to have another man accompany them on their journey and could suggest what provisions would be required, if Eli had the funds. Eli was glad of this reprieve and so introductions were made.

CHAPTER 27

Boston (Present Day)

Frank Dillon knocked on the door at 1357 Pioneer Way in Boston, Massachusetts. It was a nice door though not original to the house, Frank noticed. The house was of a typical Cape Cod-style construction: small, compact, and routinely tasteful. The front door, however, was of heavy oak, painted red with a special orifice containing uniquely contrived stained glass windows above and below the middle divider. The stained glass, both above and below, depicted scenes of the American Revolution in vivid colors. The top frame displayed George Washington crossing the Delaware River while the bottom glorified Paul Revere on his memorial ride. The glass looked professionally done and was a very impressive start to the home. Frank, who was patriotic to the core, stood for a moment studying the pictures before the door opened.

Heather Cook stood holding the door open. She appeared to be in her middle thirties and was pleasant to look at, with long blond hair pulled back into a ponytail. Her complexion was flawless, but Frank guessed she was always on the verge of losing control of her weight. Her weight at present pushed the skin of her face outward, creating that flawless complexion that immediately caught Frank's attention. Her face was round and holding a smile.

"Detective Dillon?" Heather asked, glancing at the credential Frank held in his outstretched hand. "Please come in." She gestured to the interior of the house and, after Frank passed, closed the door. She preceded Frank into the small living room of the lightly decorated home. It was as if sunshine had been invited to inhabit the room and had settled in a large square in the center of the floor, creating brilliance all around. Frank was tempted to put his sunglasses back on but considered that that might cause an awkwardness that could dull the tone of their meeting.

"You said over the phone that you were interested in some of David's things," Heather reiterated. "David is not here, he is in London attending a conference of insurance adjusters. But I know he wouldn't mind."

"I understand your husband is a relation of the Wilkes family," Frank informed. "The Eli and Rebecca Wilkes family," he clarified.

Heather went to a bookshelf against the wall of the room and withdrew a large volume. She brought it back to Frank.

"It's David's family bible," she explained. "It goes back to the early 1800s and lists all of the family ancestors, I think. Clarence and Opal Wilkes were the parents of Horace Wilkes, Rebecca's first husband. You'll find their names in the bible. Eli is listed there, although he is the end of their line. He was Rebecca and Horace's only child, and he died childless."

"Do you know anything about the family?" Frank asked.

"I believe Clarence owned a quarry in Quincy, and they cut stone that was sold around the world, but particularly in Boston. It's called the Econational Stone Works now, I think, and it's still producing stone. It's outside of Quincy about fourteen miles. Wilkes owned the quarry and the stonecutting business with a man named Orvil Clark. It was the Clark-Wilkes Quarry and Stone Cutting Company back then. They shortened their name to the C & W Stone Company in the late 1860s."

Frank grinned. "You know a lot about the family," he declared.

"I'm a schoolteacher," Heather explained. "Sixth-grade history teacher. My kids love this kind of thing, especially if you know some kind of historical family dirt. It makes the history come alive for them."

"Do you know anything about the Vanderlin treasure that Eli Wilkes was supposed to have stolen?" Frank asked hopefully.

"I've read about it," Heather responded. "I guess I don't know anything that anyone else doesn't know. Only what I've read."

"Does your husband have any family keepsakes that might go back to that time?" Frank asked. "Letters or books, a diary, or anything like that?"

Heather shook her head. "I don't know of anything like that. I've gone through most of the stuff that David has. He doesn't care about that kind of thing, but I do. I don't think his stuff goes beyond his grandparents." She paused for a second, thinking. "You know, you might try Econational. David and I went out there one time, just to see it. I think they have some kind of a library or museum on the grounds. They might have something."

Frank thanked Heather Cook for her hospitality and information and intended to do just that—drive to Quincy, Massachusetts. He arrived there just as it was getting dark and decided to stay overnight at an EconoLodge hotel. The hotel was adequate but not luxurious. On the department's budget, it was all he could hope for. The next morning, after the continental breakfast of cereal, hard-boiled eggs, and toast, Frank finished the last fourteen miles of his journey to the Econational Stone Works. The site was surrounded by a chain-link fence that must have been miles in circumference, and a large metal gate with the name displayed above it was standing open to traffic.

Inside the Works, Frank was escorted to the public relations officer, a Ms. Orenthall, who took him back to her office.

"What exactly are you looking for?" Ms. Orenthall asked. She was young, Frank observed, way too young to occupy such a position. But then everyone seemed young to him at this stage of his life, and he was continually shocked by how young the real professionals were. His doctor looked like a teenager to him, yet he discussed Frank's health with the knowledge and vocabulary of a textbook.

"I am looking for anything to do with Eli Wilkes or his mother, Rebecca Wilkes Vanderlin," Frank answered. "I understand it was Eli's grandfather, who owned the quarry at one time."

"Yes," Ms. Orenthall agreed, "he was one of the founders of the quarry." She turned and began typing on her computer keyboard. "It looks like we might have some things in the museum archives. Let's go look."

She stood and led Frank down a hallway to the back of the building, out a door and into another warehouse-type building next door. It was obvious to Frank that this was a museum of sorts since there were examples of old rock-crushing machines, pneumatic drills, diamond-tipped saws, horse-drawn wagons, and various tools. At the back of this expanse was a smaller room that was locked that, when opened, housed shelves stuffed with items. From a shelf at the back of this room, Ms. Orenthal removed a wooden box and placed it on a table nearby. She opened the box and glanced through its contents.

"This should be it," she observed. "There isn't much there. Pictures and letters is all, it looks like."

Ms. Orenthall invited Frank to sit down at the table in front of the box and to stay as long as he wanted. She would have to go back to her office to get some other work done, and he should just inform her when he was leaving so she could come back and lock the room. Frank sat down in front of the wooden box. It was not a large box, perhaps the size of a lunch box and, as Ms. Orenthall stated, contained primarily pictures and letters. Frank took the contents out of the box one by one and studied them. There were pictures of the founding fathers of the Stone Works and letters from them to various members of their families and to colleagues. There was a picture of Clarence and Opal Wilkes standing with their young son Horace Wilkes on the bank of an unknown river. It was inscribed on the back with their names and a date: 1848.

The picture of Horace and Rebecca Wilkes in a similar pose with their son Eli, who was possibly fourteen years of age at that time, caught Frank's eye. He could immediately identify Eli, even at that age, based on his resemblance to the painting that Frank had studied in the bed-and-breakfast in Elko. The picture was identified on the back as having been taken in 1863, and the background was probably California. This must have been after their estrangement from Clarence Wilkes, Frank thought. Frank felt a shiver creep up his spine and marveled at his reaction to the picture. He was not particularly a sentimental person, yet seeing the picture of Eli in a convivial setting with his parents and knowing what would befall the young man some years hence made Frank feel sad and a little lonely. It was likely not the fulfillment of his life as Eli would have imagined it at the time the picture was taken, Frank reflected.

Frank took a letter out of the box. It had not been sealed but had been folded several times. On the back of the sheet of paper was written a name in longhand: James Vanderlin! Frank turned the paper over and read the contents. It was a letter to Vanderlin from Eli Wilkes explaining why he had taken Vanderlin's watch and that he intended to post the letter when he reached Boston. Eli went on to decry Vanderlin's treatment of his mother and him and to curse Vanderlin to future despair. Eli had signed the letter at the bottom and obviously had folded it and put it in his pocket to carry to Boston where he intended to post it.

Frank sat back in the chair with the letter in front of him on the table and pondered. In a moment his eyes opened wide in understanding, and he removed the handkerchief from his pocket and wiped his forehead. A smile crept onto his lips, and he simply shook his head in astonishment. It had all been so simple, the clues leading to the discovery of Vanderlin's treasure! It had been in front of all of them all of this time!

CHAPTER 28

Wadsworth, Nevada (1872)

Eli Wilkes walked down Main Street in Wadsworth, Nevada, leading the horse he had stolen from James Vanderlin. He had just left the home of the town's doctor where Luke Proctor, the ten-year-old son of Reginald and Irene Proctor, had been taken. Eli had been introduced to the Proctors, including their other son Mark who was eight and a half, in Reno by the unnamed gentleman who had witnessed Eli's despair at having seen Angus McPhersen waiting at the Central Pacific Train Depot. Eli liked the Proctors. They were solicitous without being probing or interfering in his affairs. The Proctors had decided to forsake their dream of becoming prosperous miners when they learned how hard the labor was with so few results. They had lost most of their grubstake to an unscrupulous person in Virginia City who had sold them someone else's already recorded claim as well as the equipment to work that impossible piece of earth. Reggie had then tried to work for another miner but ended up doing all of the work while that mine owner sat by the mine entrance drinking rye all day long. After his backbreaking labor at the end of the day, Reggie would have to carry the miner back to the miner's shack and put him to bed.

The Proctors had given their farm in Missouri to their two oldest sons and had scrimped and saved just enough money to reach the gold fields of the west and to buy a modest claim. With those resources depleted and with no other marketable skill than the knowledge of farming, the Proctors decided to go back east and help their oldest sons with the family farm. They were grateful to have Eli ride along with them, although he didn't carry a gun nor did he appear to have any acumen with weapons. But he shared the loneliness of the journey with them, and his story was such that it made them grateful for their own meager misfortunes.

Unfortunately, their second-to-the-youngest son Luke took sick the first night on the trail out of Reno, and the concentration of the rest of their ride to Wadsworth was to get him to a doctor. Having found the doctor in Wadsworth, Reggie Proctor had gone to a mercantile store to secure supplies for their continued journey while Eli sat with the family for a time before going to the train station to inquire about passage east. When he was able to say good-bye to Luke, already having done so with the other Proctors, Eli left the doctor's home and began his walk to the train station. This was where he encountered a winded and hurrying Reginald Proctor coming back from the mercantile store.

"Don't go to the train station!" Reggie gushed, out of breath. "They're waiting for you there!"

"What?" Eli cried.

"I'm sorry, Eli," Reggie apologized profusely. "I was at the store and was talking to the clerk there, and I mentioned you. Not you by name, just that you had been traveling with us, and a man who must have been standing behind me overheard me and started asking questions about you. He acted all nice and such, saying that he and his friend had been waiting for you at the train station and that they were friends of yours and only wanted to help you. Now I never said your name, but he acted like he knew it was you. If these are the men you talked about then you better not go near them. This man was a rough-looking hombre, not someone you would want to tangle with."

Eli clasped his head in his hands. "Oh god!" he cried. "I'm done for! What do I do now? They'll find me and kill me!"

"You got to get out of town!" Reggie admonished. "Keep to the trail, head for the next station! Maybe you can outrun them and catch a train further down the line!"

"But I don't know how!" Eli continued plaintively. "What if there are Indians or outlaws? I don't even know how to make a fire!"

"Look, Eli!" Reggie said paternally. "I'll give you blankets and food that you can eat cold! You can live without the fire. If someone is following you, it is better without the fire anyway. Just take care of your horse! Make sure he gets fed and watered whenever you can, and keep him from injury! You can make it! Just follow the trail, you can't lose it. The wagon trains have made it, so anyone can follow it!"

Resigned to his fate, but a small measure from despair, Eli followed Reginald Proctor back to his wagon to receive the blankets and food. Eli was captured by fear and self-loathing as he received these items, which Reggie secured onto the back of Eli's saddle. Reggie walked with Eli the short distance to the edge of town and pointed the direction of the wagon trail east.

"Ride, Eli!" Reggie commanded. "Camp high on hills if you can, and watch for campfires at night. Keep alert, and above all, listen! If you hear something, or if your horse hears something, get off the trail! I believe the Humboldt River Station is about sixty or seventy miles down the way. You can be there in three or four days if you keep to the trail."

With those admonishments, Reggie slapped the back of Eli's horse, sending the horse and Eli off at a gallop out into the sage brush. Dusk was beginning to descend and seemed to keep pace with the gloom and hopelessness clouding over Eli's heart.

On his way back to the doctor's home, Reggie was confronted by the man who had interrogated him in the mercantile store. Reggie lied to the man, telling him that Eli had left Wadsworth to go back to Virginia City to reconcile with his stepfather, but he could see the suspicion and disbelief in the man's eyes. Reggie felt an overwhelming sadness for Eli Wilkes as he walked into the doctor's home/office sitting room and embraced Irene to her pleased surprise.

CHAPTER 29

Elko, Nevada (Present Day)

Frank Dillon took a night flight back to Elko from Boston. While waiting for the plane to depart, Frank called Michelle Neubrander from his cell phone.

"I've got news!" Frank began as soon as Michelle answered.

"So do I!" Michelle parried.

"Okay . . . then you first," Frank decided.

"Guess who is a Vanderlin descendant and forgot to mention it!" Michelle stated triumphantly. Then, without waiting for Frank's reply, "Vincent Lowler!"

There was silence for a second.

"Did you hear me?" Michelle questioned. "Vincent Lowler is related to the rest of them!"

"How did you find that out?" Frank asked.

Michelle's voice was loaded with pride and excitement. "The Mormons!" she exclaimed. "They keep extensive genealogical records. I got on their genealogical website, requested the

Vanderlin family tree, and 'Lowler' came up along with the rest of them!"

"Very good!" Frank was impressed.

Michelle wished that she could see Frank's face, to see the expression of pride and astonishment that she could hear in his voice. She felt like she finally contributed something to the investigation. Perhaps she had turned a corner and was becoming a valuable member of the team.

"What was your news?" she asked, remembering the second part of their opening greeting.

"Hold on, Michelle. They're making an announcement over the loudspeaker!" Frank held up his hand as if Michelle could see the stop signal. "Oops! Got to go! They're boarding my flight!" With that, he closed up the phone, picked up his bag, and got in the line that was forming to board the airplane.

While Frank was flying from Boston to Salt Lake City where he would transfer to an excursion arm of Delta Airlines for the last leg of his trip to Elko, Andy Walch snuck out of the Stockmen's Hotel and walked east down the street and over a block to the Dancin & Diddlin bordello. He didn't want either the Ryder siblings or his police shadow to know where he was going. It wasn't that he was doing anything illegal since prostitution in Nevada outside of Clark County and Washoe County was legal and regulated. Because of the legal prostitution in the rest of the state, apart from those counties noted, there was very little street prostitution. Oppositely, in Las Vegas and Reno, street prostitution was flourishing, as was AIDS and other sexually transmitted diseases, because the activity was not regulated other than making it illegal.

Andy was ashamed of going to a bordello, but he was equally excited to be doing something that society has deemed an aberration. He fantasized that sex with a prostitute was far more exotic and exciting than sex with a partner with whom a relationship had been nurtured and cultivated. Sex with a prostitute did not require reciprocation. His demands, and his alone, were all that anyone was interested in. It was a relief to be sexually satisfied in that way, without having the guilt of another's expectations. Yet society had declared this activity to be morally corrupt and reprehensible, that to be intimate with a prostitute was an abomination to God and worthy of a fiery afterlife. Thus, as Andy entered the bordello and watched the girls line up in front of him for his inspection and selection, he felt the rush of both guilt and excitement.

When the "immoral" act was accomplished to Andy's satisfaction, he left the bordello, the tingling sensation of sexual fulfillment and moral flaunting lingering in his body. It was dark on that street with only the neon signs of the three or four bordellos to light the way back to the block occupied by the Stockmen's Hotel and Casino. At the corner of River and Third Streets, several large trees were connected by an enormously high hedge of ill-managed bushes. There was a breeze, as was common in Elko, and the foliage rustled and spoke with the language of the forest.

As Andy passed the corner where the darkness of the trees and bushes brought the jungle to the city, a movement caught the corner of Andy's attention. Then he felt a sudden pain in his side and a rupturing feeling in his chest. As he looked down, a long knife was being withdrawn from between his ribs, and the carrier of this knife simply faded back into the darkness of the foliage along the street. Andy's legs buckled, acting of their own volition, and Andy was flung to the ground, his knees convulsing up to his chest. He tried to call for help, but nothing but gurgling came out of his mouth. His lungs filled with blood, and as he gasped harder and longer for each breath, Andy Walch slowly died of asphyxiation.

Andy's body was found lying on the corner under the trees by an elderly woman walking her dog just as Frank's plane was touching down in Elko. After being contacted by dispatch, Frank drove the short distance directly to that spot. The first responding officer had cordoned off both River and Third Streets with police tape and was assisting in moving what little traffic happened at that time of night to other streets. Michelle pulled up in her department vehicle shortly after Frank's arrival. She sidled in beside Frank without him giving any indication that he had noticed her.

"Andy?" she asked, already knowing the answer.

"It's him," Frank acknowledged.

"What was he doing here?" Michelle questioned, staring down at the body. Frank nodded meaningfully in the direction of the bordellos. "Did anyone else know where he was going?" Michelle continued.

"Apparently not," Frank answered. "He didn't tell the watch officer or the Ryders, just snuck out."

Michelle shook her head in confusion and anger.

"Why on earth would he do that?" she cried, exasperated.

Frank shrugged. "A man's got to do what a man's got to do, I guess." Michelle glanced at Frank to see if he was smiling at this comment. His expression had not changed, but the absurdity of the situation did create a smile in his mind. Becoming serious again and to add meaning to his comment, Frank added, "Sometimes you can't know why people do the things they do. I suspect that Andy didn't want anyone to know where he was going because he was ashamed of his need for it."

"His need for what?" Michelle asked, still glancing at Frank and already knowing the answer.

"Sex!" Frank responded in surprise, thinking his meaning was clear.

"Men!" Michelle commented, turning a disparaging eye back to the inert body of Andy Walch. "I'll never understand why men live so for sex, as if there is nothing else worthwhile in life. Can't you all see beyond that?"

Frank laughed sincerely.

"It's a basic need, Michelle, like eating or sleeping. We all feel it, women as well as men. It's instinctual to all of us. It happens in men a little differently than in women, that's all. Generally with women, sex is accompanied or preceded by other things, like love or security. The instinct in men is to procreate, to spread the seed of life as often and in as many places as possible."

"But that's just stupid!" Michelle argued. "That's why our world is becoming so overpopulated! Because men can't keep it in their pants!"

"Well you are right about that!" Frank agreed. "But it is no more stupid than a dog trying to kick up dirt after pissing in the grass. Half the time they're kicking up dirt in the opposite direction, nowhere near where they pissed. They do it because it's instinct. They don't know why they're doing it. It's an instinct left over from a time when it made sense, when covering one's scent meant survival. It's not needed anymore, but nevertheless, there it is."

Michelle was not done with the argument. "If sex is so instinctual and so important, why didn't God make it the same in women as in men? That would make sense! Then it wouldn't be such a complete mess, and we wouldn't be fighting all the time!"

Again, Frank laughed. "It would certainly be easier nowadays if that were the case. Back in the day though, when the world needed to be populated and survival came in numbers and groups, monogamy probably wasn't as mandated as it is now. Protection came in tribing up, and the more people in the tribe the better. Women were probably grateful that men were running around making more kids back then. Unfortunately, the circumstances have changed, but the instinct hasn't."

"Well I just think it's all messed up!" Michelle concluded.

"That it is, that it is," Frank capitulated. Then he added with sarcasm: "Fortunately today, we have religion to keep us on the straight and narrow and to tell us that we are going to hell if we don't keep our instincts in check."

"A lot of good that's done us!" Michelle countered.

Frank nodded down at Andy Walch. "I suspect he would agree with you about now. If he could have dealt with that guilt and told someone where he was going, he would probably be alive right now."

Michelle shrugged.

"So what now?" she asked. "Where do we go from here?"

"What did you find out about the people in the bed-and-breakfast and those hired at the Stockmen's in the last couple of weeks?" Frank inquired.

"There was nothing unusual about the people at the bed-and-breakfast. They've lived here for years and had no reason to kill anyone. One of the maids at the Stockmen's was born here. The other maid, Sylvia Sanchez, and the maintenance worker, Juan Ortega, I think are both illegal. They don't speak English and have no documents, so I couldn't find out anything about them. I did ask for info from Homeland Security, INS, but I don't expect to hear anything back for a while. I doubt they'll have anything on those two either, other than they're illegal."

Frank nodded, satisfied. "I think we know who did this, and I think I know why," he stated emphatically. "I want to set a little trap and see what happens. We're going to need Jason Ryder's help though."

Michelle looked at Frank, stunned, and waited for his explanation.

CHAPTER 30

Humboldt River (1872)

Eli Wilkes sat in the bushes sobbing quietly. It was difficult to stifle the sobs. There was no moon, and it was an especially dark night. Yet Eli could see the bodies strewn around the campfire, their grotesque images revealed by the flickering light of the dying embers. The two men there had offered Eli food and coffee earlier that very evening, and he had gratefully accepted. They were brothers, these two—Mormon boys on their way back to their father's ranch on the edge of the Ruby Mountains. They had been kind to Eli, noting quickly his inexperience with the environment in which they found themselves. He had eaten their food greedily, and they had smiled to each other, glad in their ability to offer service.

They had invited Eli to stay the night, to camp next to their fire for its warmth and promise of coffee in the morning, but Eli felt he must go on. Eli knew he wouldn't go far; in fact, he would stay close enough to see the glow of the fire in the darkness. But he would camp out in the darkness. He was being followed; of that he was certain. He took seriously the admonition of Reggie Proctor that he should not use a fire, that he was better protected by the darkness.

Eli was right to decline the invitation of the brothers. He had ridden but a short distance in the growing darkness when he decided to lay out his bedroll and get some sleep. He was awakened before long by gunshots. The sounds of the gunshots reverberated across his ears, drawing him instantly to awareness. He listened in the night air intently for what seemed like hours until he could hear horses coming his way. Eli left his bedroll and crept to his horse, which was tied nearby. He held his horse's head tightly, not wanting the animal to make any sound as the sounds of other horses came close and then gradually distanced away.

Eli trembled finally as he let go of the tight grip he had on his horse. What to do? Should he go back and see what had become of the Mormon brothers? Should he go on? In going on, he might run into the men who had created the recent sounds, sounds of movement and of violence. He would go back! But what if someone was still there waiting for him or the others? Eli shook with his dilemma, banging his head with his fists in frustration. He had no skill in this sort of thing! He literally did not know what to do!

He could stay where he was for the moment—in other words, do nothing! He could wait for a time and then go back or go on. He could wait and listen! That would probably be the advice that Reggie would give him. He decided that was what he would do; he would wait alertly! And this he did for several hours. Finally, Eli knew that he had to do something more. He wanted to go back to help the brothers if he could, and he was tired of waiting. He was cold, and he knew he would not sleep more that night. Eli left his horse tied where it was and crept back to the camp of his earlier companions.

Cast by the edge of the light from the last vestiges of fire, Eli could see that the brothers were dead. The younger one, Joseph, lay twisted on his side and back, the back of his shirt stained with blood. Brigham, the older one who was only nineteen, lay on his stomach pointed away from the fire. It appeared that he had tried to run and had been shot in the back. Their horses were gone, and their belongings were strewn about. They had been murdered and robbed, probably not even noticing their murderers until the first shots were fired. By then it was too late.

Eli sat on his haunches at the edge of the light and shivered uncontrollably. He knew without a doubt that the monsters who had done this were the same men tracking him. In the morning light, they would discover that they had lost his trail and would backtrack to find it again. They would come back to the camp of the Mormon brothers and start over again. Or perhaps they had figured out what Eli was trying to do. It shouldn't be hard to discern. He was obviously following the line of the wagons and the train. They could simply go to the next train station at Humboldt River and wait for him. It became clear to Eli that he couldn't go to Humboldt River Station—that if he stayed on his path, he would have to skirt the station in order to survive. But how would he live if he couldn't resupply at the station?

The only reasonable thing to do was to go through the Mormon brothers' things to see if there was anything he could use. And this he did, right there in the beginnings of morning light. He found no weapons, and anything of monetary value was gone or had never been there. He did find foodstuffs and another usable blanket. Eli was encouraged by his finds, thinking that he might be able to survive using the advice of Reggie Proctor and the largess of the Mormon brothers. The idea of going through the belongings of the recently dead, especially those who had been so kind to him, bothered Eli significantly. Yet he did it and later was proud that he had. Perhaps he was not as useless as he imagined. Perhaps he would make it to Boston to rest in the bosom and protection of his paternal grandfather.

CHAPTER 31

Elko, Nevada (Present Day)

Vincent Lowler sat at his desk in his office in the basement of the bed-and-breakfast house on Silver Street. He was going through bills and paying them via the Internet on his computer. He was switching back and forth between his bill-paying program and a website in Virginia City that detailed the life of James Vanderlin. There were not that many sites on the Internet that dealt with James Vanderlin. Vincent had discovered his descendence from the Vanderlin family when he was twenty-two and attending his final year at the University of Nevada in Las Vegas. He had been doing research on his own family tree, and at the time, the Vanderlin connection meant nothing to him. During the next few years, however, he had delved more deeply into the particular histories of his ancestors, looking for some kind of distinction that he could claim as his own, and discovered James Vanderlin's notoriety. James Vanderlin was the Jessie James, the Ivan the Terrible, the Blackbeard of the Lowler family tree.

Unfortunately, very little was detailed about James Vanderlin. Only two or three descendants of the Vanderlins had tried to write biographies of James, and those biographies always settled around the darkness surrounding the killing of Eli Wilkes and the hidden Vanderlin treasure. This connection was what made Vanderlin worth writing about and worth researching. Yet there was very little material to go on. Nothing was written of James's early life, and only a few mentions of him could be located after he moved to Virginia City. The biographies from Vanderlin descendants mostly witnessed folklore passed down from generation to generation within the Vanderlin family.

The *Virginia City Enterprise* was the principal background source regarding Vanderlin through its obituary of his death in the great 1875 conflagration of that city. It alluded to previous articles written regarding James's notoriety that were destroyed in that 1875 fire, one or two by Samuel Clemens himself. That obituary, which gave some detail of James's suspected involvement in the killing of his stepson and implied several of his other notorious activities, and the family's verbal stories of Vanderlin's exploits were the totality of his knowledge of James Vanderlin. Still, Vincent Lowler continued to explore the Internet looking for tidbits that carried the Vanderlin name. His interest was not in creating another biography of James Vanderlin but in finding Vanderlin's lost treasure. Through the years, he had become obsessed with this project to the point of buying the house that was the scene of Eli Wilkes's demise. He had systematically renovated the entire house, ostensibly to bring it back to the time period of Eli's death, but his real intention was to look for the treasure or clues to its location.

All of his efforts to recover the treasure had been in vain. While the "bed-and-breakfast as a destination" concept had been fairly successful financially, Vincent was frustrated with the final desired result. Sometimes he felt no closer to the treasure than he was when he had purchased the home. And this latest trouble perplexed him to an intolerable extent. He didn't know of the Vanderlin descendants' intended reunion in his bed-and-breakfast establishment until they arrived and proclaimed their relationship. At first he had secretly laughed at their amateurish inclinations and debates, for these were not even the prominent Vanderlin descendants. Not even one of these people had done adequate research or had contributed to a biography of James Vanderlin! They were strictly here on a lark, the brainstorm of the Ryder woman. As if they could find anything remotely relating to the Vanderlin treasure!

Except for Benjamin Dulles. He was a surprise to Vincent. Benjamin came down the stairs to the basement that fateful day and began asking questions about the painting of Eli Wilkes: probing questions, good questions. Benjamin Dulles was not stupid like the rest of that group. Benjamin had guessed that the painting was a message to James Vanderlin from Eli Wilkes, a message that James Vanderlin never got because he never came to the house on Silver Street. Benjamin had been to the museum in Virginia City and had seen the watch that Eli had inscribed to James. He had figured out that the watch led back to the painting in Vincent's drawing room. Benjamin was close to discovering something, something that he refused to disclose to Vincent. Vincent himself had gotten that far in the puzzle but could not seem to get any further. But Benjamin—Benjamin seemed to be on the verge of discovering the truth, and by that the treasure! That was what was intolerable! To think that this amateur, this interloper who had done nothing to deserve the prize—who had not spent a lifetime searching, planning, and reaching—was about to discover the object of a lifetime's desire. Why, it was unfair and unfathomable!

Vincent turned and stared at the painting of Eli Wilkes that now leaned against the table in his office/kitchen. Perhaps it had been a mistake to hang it in the drawing room after he had renovated the house; it drew too much attention. Yet that had been the whole point of the destination bed-and-breakfast, the very thing that financed Vincent's obsession! The painting was the centerpiece of that concept and had to be available for everyone to gaze at! Now, however, with the bed-and-breakfast being temporarily out of service, Vincent saw no need to leave the painting in such a vulnerable place as the drawing room.

Vincent's attention was diverted by the sound of the door at the top of the stairs opening. He could hear footsteps on the stairs and shook his head in irritation. Now what? he pondered. He turned the painting to face the table and opened his apartment door. There stood Frank Dillon and Michelle Neubrander. Vincent's face registered surprise.

"What's happened?" he asked hurriedly.

"What hasn't happened!" Frank Dillon responded, pushing past Vincent and into the apartment. Vincent shrugged and opened the door further to allow Michelle Neubrander to enter as well.

"We came over to look at that painting in your lounge and found that it was no longer there!" Frank admonished.

Vincent turned red-faced to stand next to the painting, which was placed with its back to Frank and Michelle.

"I took it down!" he stated defensively. "Since you won't allow me to have any guests, I didn't want to leave the painting upstairs where anyone could take it!"

"I see," Frank said. Looking at the back of the painting, Frank asked, "Is that it?"

Vincent nodded and turned the picture around.

"Um!" Frank muttered, studying the picture as he had before. "I'm afraid we're going to have to impound the picture as evidence!"

"What!" chortled Vincent. "You can't! I mean, you mustn't! It's mine! It's not evidence!" He began pleading. "I'll keep it here for you! I'll lock it up! You can see it anytime you need to! Please don't take it!" He was practically crying. Frank put both hands on Vincent's arms and moved him back to the sink.

"Now, now Vincent! It will be safe! Don't worry, nothing will happen to it! It will be locked in a vault until this whole thing is settled! It will be safer than here!" Frank said this in an unruffled paternal tone, which seemed to have a calming effect on Vincent.

"But why now? Why after all this time and after all that's happened?" Vincent asked, sincerely confused.

"Ah!" Frank responded. "That is the thing, isn't it? Well, it turns out that Jason Ryder believes he knows the answer to all of this. He is going to come down to the station tomorrow morning and tell us what this is all about! He says the painting is the key to what has happened here! Apparently, Benjamin Dulles told him some things about the painting that Jason had forgotten or didn't understand until now, and he believes he has figured out the rest of the puzzle regarding the Vanderlin treasure! He believes it will clear up the entire mess!"

Vincent stood there in complete astonishment, unable to utter a word. Frank simply stood there looking at the floor, nodding as if lost in his own thoughts and his own astonishment.

"But why wait 'til tomorrow?" Vincent asked the obvious question finally.

"Ah!" Frank answered again. "That's a good question. Apparently, Jason wants to run the whole thing by his sister and his grandmother to see if it makes sense to them, and his grandmother lives in Illinois, which is a couple hours later, and goes to bed early. Apparently, he doesn't want to wake her."

"That's ridiculous!" Vincent uttered.

Frank smiled and gave Michelle a knowing glance, which Vincent caught.

"We tend to agree with you, Vincent!" Frank said. "But with what little we have to go on, and if there is any possibility of it being true, we're willing to wait the few hours to see! He believes he can show us on the painting itself the solution to the entire business! That's why we have to take it into evidence!"

"I see," said Vincent as if he didn't.

Vincent did not argue any more to save his painting from being removed. He stood aside and let them leave, painting in hand. He sat for several hours on the divan with his head cupped in his hands and thought and cried. He felt trapped, urged on, and fatefully purposed. What could he do? What else could he do? It just did not seem fair that he was compelled to this. To have come this far, to have done what he had done! He could not stop; he could not step back! It was a matter of deserving! He deserved it! He deserved it all! Not them!

At around midnight, Vincent roused himself, washed his face, and dressed himself entirely in black clothing to include his black rubber-soled shoes. He left the bed-and-breakfast on Silver Street and walked the short distance to the Stockman's Hotel on Commercial Street. He entered by one of the backdoors and wound his way to the kitchen of the hotel's café. Checking quickly to make certain no one was there, he secured one of the kitchen cutting knives and made his way to the backstairs. He traversed the stairway to the top floor and opened the door slowly, quietly, peering down the hallway. The police guard was not sitting in his chair in the hallway! That was disturbing!

Vincent passed through the doorway and moved quickly down the hallway. He quietly opened the far door at the other end of the hallway and peered into the main stairway. The guard was sitting on the top carpeted stair, leaning against the wall, a burned-down cigarette dangling in his limp hand resting on the carpet. The guard had gone into the stairway for a cigarette and had fallen asleep! Unbelievable luck, Vincent thought. He quietly closed the hall door and crept to the two doors closest to the guard's chair where Vincent believed the Ryder siblings would be sleeping. Which room, he wondered? For some reason, Vincent felt that the guard would sit with his chair against Elizabeth Ryder's wall, facing Jason Ryder's room. It seemed more protective of Elizabeth Ryder, which Vincent believed a guard would reason. He knelt by the doorknob of the opposite room and began manipulating the lock with lock picks he had brought with him. Soon, the door gave way into the room.

Vincent could hear snores—manly snores—and believed he had found Jason Ryder's room. He moved silently to the bed and, with a harsh downward swing, stabbed the form there with the kitchen knife. Oddly, the knife met little resistance from the form. Just then, the room was flooded in light, and as Vincent shielded his eyes with his arm, he saw the figures of men in uniform pouring into the room from the bathroom and hallway!

CHAPTER 32

Winnemucca, Nevada (1872)

From where he stood against the outside wall of the livery stable, Eli Wilkes could peer around the wooden structure and have a clear view of the train station. Eli looked ragged. He hadn't bathed in over a week's time, and his clothes had been slept in for the past several days. His clothes had trail dirt on them that he would normally have had dusted in the bathhouse of the town or have washed away in a stream that he would pass. But he hadn't stopped in Humboldt River Station as he had originally planned, nor had he passed any water in the wretched desert before reaching the area of Humboldt River Station. He had been too afraid. Humboldt River Station was small, and the men following him could easily pick up his trail leading out of the town even if he could have hidden from them while there. He did have a change of clothing, but he hadn't bothered to make use of them. Besides, they were dirty as well, having not been washed since leaving the Proctors.

Eli kept a sharp eye out for any movement around him. He stood inside a small outdoor stable area next to the main stable building. The fence that he leaned against to peer around the building was covered in a coarse wool horse blanket, and there were others around the fence drying in the afternoon sun. The blankets served Eli's purpose as a small fort hiding him from the prying eyes of those walking nearby. It gave him an advantage in being able to watch the train station discreetly. Eli had been there for some minutes—perhaps an hour or more. He wanted more than anything to be able to walk into the train station and purchase a ticket for as far as his money would take him. Yet he knew it was possible that the men his stepfather employed might still be following him. It was likely. Eli was certain that his stepfather had offered a large sum of money to the man that would bring his precious treasure back to him. And these kinds of men were very motivated by money.

Then Eli saw him: Joe Bide! Bide stepped from the main entrance to the train station and rolled a cigarette, lit it, and began inhaling the smoke while he leaned against the post of the station's porch. Eli jerked back to the safety of the corral, crestfallen. It would be as before! He would never get to Boston!

When Eli looked again, two other men had joined Bide. They were equally rough looking and stood there smoking with Bide as if there was no concern in the world. One actually laughed heartily at some spoken joke or word. Eli didn't recognize the other men, but he had no doubt that they worked for James Vanderlin as well. Bide was a special creature who had gone out of his way to torment Eli whenever he saw Eli outside the presence of Eli's mother or Vanderlin. He obviously detested Eli and made suggestive comments and bodily gestures with his hands and torso. Another man joined the three, and all went back into the train station.

Eli slid down the wall of the stable and sat in the noxious dirt, cradling his head in his forearms. He had counted on

Winnemucca being a refuge from the past turmoil. It was far enough away from Virginia City that he should have been safe. Vanderlin must have offered an enormous sum to the mercenaries to cause them to continue so ardently. Eli was well aware that he could not ride his horse all of the way to Boston. He would have to catch the train somewhere along the way, and he knew he would run out of money if he didn't catch the train soon. Every time he needed supplies, he had to spend what he had stolen. If this kept up, there would be a time when he wouldn't have enough funds left to purchase the ticket all of the way to Boston. Then what would he do? What if his horse became injured or died from some ailment or was stolen?

Eli's plight felt hopeless. He couldn't stay here, and he couldn't imagine going on. The only advantage was that Winnemucca was big enough that it afforded some anonymity—at least for a time. In any town this side of St. Louis, Eli would ultimately be discovered, especially with the resources that James Vanderlin could command. His only hope was to go on, to continue east; and obviously, that would not be by train. At least not from this town. The next station was at Carlin just west of Carlin Canyon. And then there was Elko, a slightly larger town than Carlin and twenty some miles beyond with a little more potential to be anonymous. Beyond that were Humboldt Wells, Toano, Montello, Matlin, Monument, Promontory, and then Ogden above the Salt Lake Valley. Eli knew that, without help, he would not last beyond the next few stations.

Then Eli was hit with an inspiration. He would wire to his grandfather in Boston for help and money and pick up his grandfather's response in Elko where he was certain there would be a telegraph office. He would ride to Elko, skirting Carlin just in case someone waited there for him, and hopefully catch the train from Elko. It would be about a week's ride to Elko on horseback, although he might be able to catch a stagecoach outside of Winnemucca and ride it the distance to Elko. Once outside of town, he had a better chance on a stage than on horseback, especially in the company of others. This then was what he would do.

CHAPTER 33

Elko (Present Day)

Vincent Lowler sat in a chair in a conference room at the Stockmen's Hotel, leaning with his elbows on a long folding table, his face hidden in his hands. He was mute and practically catatonic. An officer in uniform sat in a chair next to the only door, his arms crossing his chest, staring at Vincent with a smug expression on his face. The officer was a gigantic man whose muscled arms stretched the short-sleeved uniform that clung to his biceps. His expression intimated that he hoped Vincent would try to do something foolish, like escape. It would be the opportunity of a lifetime, to bend the little man into a pretzel of contortion with very little effort on the officer's part. That, of course, did not happen, for Vincent was truly caught. And in Vincent's mind, he did not see any alternative other than to accept his fate and declare his culpability.

Frank Dillon entered the room carrying two cups of coffee, followed by Michelle Neubrander who not only carried a cup of coffee but was sipping at it as she entered. Frank sat opposite

Vincent at the table and pushed one of the cups across to him. Michelle sat next to Frank.

"Well," said Frank matter-of-factly, "where shall we begin?"

Vincent sat up and shrugged as he reached out and took the cup of coffee.

"I did it," he said almost casually, with resignation tingeing his voice. "I killed him."

"Who?" Frank asked carefully.

"Benjamin Dulles, of course!" Vincent chimed with a touch of irritation. "Who else?"

"Ah! Who else indeed!" Frank responded.

Elizabeth and Jason Ryder stood outside the conference room, leaning against a wall, surrounded by uniformed officers who had participated in the earlier charade and trap. They were milling about and talking in excited whispers. None of the officers had previously participated in something so exciting or as productive in importance. They had all been part of drug raids in the city and its environs and had slammed into houses for which search warrants had been obtained, guns drawn and loudly ordering any inhabitants to surrender. But they had never participated in anything this important: to trap and capture a serial killer. This was something that they could brag about to their children and grandchildren.

The excitement and hushed clamor stopped abruptly as the conference room door opened and Frank Dillon exited the room. He walked directly to Elizabeth and Jason.

"Well, he's confessed to Benjamin's murder," Frank answered the questioning look from both Elizabeth and Jason. "We wouldn't have been able to do this without your help. The department owes you a debt of gratitude."

Both Elizabeth and Jason exhaled a sigh of relief, and Elizabeth quietly began sobbing into a handkerchief.

"So it's finally over?" Jason asked while putting his arm around his sister comfortingly.

"I hope so," Frank said somewhat hesitantly. And then in answer to Jason's questioning glance, he added, "Lowler hasn't admitted to the other murders yet, but I think it is just a matter of time. We are going to take him down to the jail and book him in on the one murder. We'll add the others when we've had a chance to work on him. I'm sure he will confess to them too."

"Did he say why?" Elizabeth asked, dabbing at her eyes with the handkerchief.

"Ah, yes," Frank responded. "Apparently, Vincent felt Benjamin was getting too close to the treasure of James Vanderlin. I don't think you knew, but Vincent was related to the Vanderlins as well."

Both Elizabeth and Jason stepped back in surprise.

"The day Benjamin was killed, he went down to Vincent's apartment to question Vincent about the painting. He had figured out something but wouldn't tell Vincent what. Vincent followed him upstairs and killed him," Frank continued.

"Had Benjamin figured anything out?" Elizabeth asked.

Frank shook his head. "I don't know."

"Did Vincent find the treasure?" Jason queried.

"I don't think he figured it out," Frank said with an enigmatic smile. "Well, we have to get Vincent to the jail."

With that, Frank turned and walked back into the conference room. He had Vincent stand and had the officer guarding the door put handcuffs on Vincent. With Vincent's arms securely fastened behind his back, Frank and Michelle escorted him back out the door and into the hallway where the Ryders and the milling police officers still stood, followed by the gigantic officer who wanted to make sure he received his handcuffs back. Elizabeth watched Vincent's face as he walked by, hoping to discern from Vincent's expression some idea of remorse or understanding of why Vincent had done such horrible things. Vincent neither acknowledged the Ryder siblings nor any of the other officers standing in the hallway. He walked past them with his head hung down, a tear dropping from his left eye. If Elizabeth could have known, this tear was not any recognition on Vincent's part of wrongdoing but was simply the end result of his frustration of having been thwarted in his quest for his lifelong desire. Vincent was feeling for the first time, though still not believing, that he would never be able to hold the Vanderlin gold in his hands.

Having passed through the crowd of officers and the Ryders in the hallway, Frank could see at the end of the hall a door that led to the back of the hotel and the alleyway beyond. A police vehicle with a corrugated metal partition in the backseat would be waiting there to take Vincent to the jail. After Vincent was booked into the jail on the single count of murder, Frank would continue the interrogation to complete the rest of the murders. Halfway down the hall, a maintenance worker was kneeling down at the wall working on an electrical outlet. As Frank, Vincent, and Michelle began to pass the worker, the worker stood with his back to the wall to allow them to pass and to observe the passing. Frank glanced at the maintenance worker, and a moment of recognition crossed his mind.

As Vincent, with Frank and Michelle on either side, passed the worker, the maintenance worker stepped out into the hall behind the trio, rushed up to Vincent from behind, and began stabbing Vincent in the back with a screwdriver. Blood spurted from the body of Vincent, whose legs immediately buckled, and Vincent sank out of the arms of both Frank and Michelle to fall writhing to the hallway floor. Michelle, who thought that Vincent had merely stumbled, tried to catch him before he hit the floor but managed only to turn him onto his back, spreading the blood across and into the rich gold-colored carpet of the hallway. The gigantic officer who had been following several steps behind Frank and Michelle grabbed the maintenance worker, who seemed a very small man compared to the giant in whose arms he was encircled, and threw him facedown to the floor. The officer immediately twisted the maintenance worker's arm into an armlock and placed his knee on the worker's neck holding him securely to the floor. Several more officers rushed up to help secure the maintenance worker and to place him in handcuffs.

The mayhem in the hallway was astounding. Officers had run down the hall and had surrounded the gigantic officer and his prey, shoving the Ryder siblings against the wall as they rushed by and knocking Elizabeth to the floor. Elizabeth scraped her elbow against the wall as she was shoved out of the way and fell to the floor. Her elbow immediately began bleeding, staining her long-sleeved white blouse. Seeing the blood, Jason grabbed his sister protectively and held her in his arms, covering her body with his until the final officer had passed by.

Vincent Lowler's body went into its final death throes, lightly convulsing and shaking on the floor until he finally lay limp and unresponding. Frank and Michelle had stained the knees of their pants kneeling in Vincent's blood while they tried to fend off the final mortality, but to no avail. By the color of the blood oozing from Vincent's body, Frank could tell that his liver and kidneys had been penetrated. Their attempts at cardio resuscitation were futile, and Vincent Lowler expired before their eyes.

Frank stood shakily and walked back to the milieu of officers. He parted them and looked down at the angel of Vincent Lowler's death, the earlier hint of recognition now registering clearly in his mind.

CHAPTER 34

Elko, Nevada (1872)

It was over for Eli Wilkes. He had just left the telegraph office in Elko. There had been no reply from his grandfather to Eli's urgent request for help. Eli's mind was spinning and, after leaving the telegraph office, he had almost run straight into Will Tenerette, one of his stepfather's henchmen. Luckily for Eli, Tenerette had been looking the other way as he entered the saloon next to the telegraph office. Eli had ducked back into the telegraph office and waited until he could slip out and around the building to run the distance to a small bathhouse down the alleyway. He had stood inside the mudroom of that building, his body shaking from fear and exertion.

Eli did not have enough money left to make it beyond Promontory or Ogden at the farthest by train or stagecoach. That meant he would have to ride the rest of the way east on the horse he had stolen from James Vanderlin. But the stage driver had noted a limp in Eli's horse after he had let Eli off the stage just outside of Elko. Eli had not dared to ride the horse any further and had walked the last miles into Elko leading the horse. And if the horse was not so seriously injured and could be ridden east, would his grandfather accept Eli into his household? His failure to reply to Eli's telegram bode ill for Eli's prospects in that direction.

Perhaps Eli could go to Tenerette and whoever else was hunting him in Elko and make a deal to return Vanderlin's property. Perhaps he could return to Virginia City and make amends with his stepfather. Unlikely. Eli had seen the way Vanderlin dealt with people who had displeased him, and Eli had never pleased him. Eli was certain that Vanderlin had issued a death warrant on him and was willing to pay handsomely that it be executed effectively. These men would not be reasoned with other than with money, and Eli had not enough.

Eli sat down on his haunches in the mudroom of that bathhouse and finally realized his futility. Oddly enough, that realization brought a certain peace to Eli: a resignation. He finally stood with the resolution of his fate and began planning the next small block of his life. He wanted to have an impact on James Vanderlin. He wanted this not to be a triumph for Vanderlin. He wanted to be remembered by someone even if not for the right reasons. Instinctively, he took out the pocket watch that he had stolen from James Vanderlin, opened it, and looked at it for the first time since this journey began. An idea began to emerge in Eli's mind.

Eli took out the remainder of the cash and coin that he had left and counted it. He had passed by a bordello on his walk into town and thought instantly of that house. Perhaps he could stay there for a couple of days while he accomplished the plan that had formulated in his mind. Someone at that house could probably refer him to a portrait artist and to an engraver, and perhaps he would have enough money left over to enjoy the comfort of a woman.

Eli smiled as he left the mudroom and continued down the alleyway as far as it would take him.

CHAPTER 35

Elko (Present Day)

Elizabeth Ryder stood in what appeared to be a training room at the Elko County jail. The room was large and had whiteboards on the walls interspersed with posters depicting virtuous ideals like leadership and teamwork. A jail nurse stood next to her, applying antiseptic and a bandage to Elizabeth's elbow. Jason Ryder stood opposite them with his back to them, his eyes studying one of the posters on the wall. He appeared enraptured with the poster, but in reality, his mind was whirling with recent images of blood and chaos. They had been brought to the jail by one of the officers in a police vehicle at the request of Frank Dillon who had stayed behind at the Stockmen's Hotel to assist the paramedics and then the medical examiner with the remains of Vincent Lowler. Nothing could be done for Vincent who had died in a pool of his own blood.

Frank observed the removal of the maintenance worker in a police vehicle to the county jail and, after conferring with the medical examiner, followed the crowd to the jail. He arrived at the tail end of the booking process for the maintenance worker, shadowed this whole time by Michelle Neubrander. He arranged for an interview room to be available in the booking area for himself, Michelle, and the maintenance worker after the booking process had been completed and then, having interviewed the maintenance worker, went upstairs to talk to the Ryder siblings.

By the time Frank arrived at the training room upstairs in the jail, Elizabeth and Jason were sharing a can of soda and whispering between themselves about what had happened. They came to alert attention when Frank entered the room and sat at the table in front of them.

"Can I get you something?" Frank asked indulgently. "I see you already have something to drink."

Elizabeth shook her head, her eyes quizzical. Jason shook his head in agreement.

"How is your arm?" Frank asked, looking at the bloodstained sleeve of Elizabeth's blouse. "Was it bad?"

Again, Elizabeth shook her head. "I'm all right."

"Good," Frank replied and sat back in his chair, stretching his legs out under the table. "I am releasing the two of you to go home. But before you go, I wanted to give you the whole picture of this sordid mess as we have put it together. I think you deserve at least that."

Both Elizabeth and Jason nodded expectantly.

Frank continued in the same tone. "I also wanted to thank you for being patient this past week or so. I know this ordeal cannot have been pleasant for you and that you were probably scared a good portion of the time."

Again, the Ryder siblings nodded, waiting.

"Let me not keep you in suspense and get right to the essential points," Frank declared. "Vincent Lowler killed Benjamin Dulles. He acted alone and did it because he thought Benjamin was getting too close to finding the Vanderlin treasure. Apparently, Lowler had been obsessed with the treasure for a long time and was not about to let anyone surpass him in its discovery."

"What about the others?" Jason and Elizabeth chimed together.

"Ah yes," Frank responded. "The others. That was the work of Izzy Dulles."

The expression of shock on the faces of both Elizabeth and Jason brought further explanation from Frank.

"Izzy Dulles took her son back to Michigan and returned to Elko almost immediately. She came back in the guise of a part-time maintenance worker named Juan Ortiz and got a job at the Stockmen's Hotel where she could do her damnedest to the rest of your party at her own leisure. Back in Michigan, she worked as a Spanish and theater arts teacher at a home for juvenile delinquents. It was not that difficult for her to come here and pass herself off as an illegal Mexican worker who spoke no English. Her Spanish was excellent, and her 'illegal' status stopped people from delving too deeply into her story. No one seemed to question the fact that she was not a man, but her theatre experience probably helped there."

"But why would she want to kill us?" Elizabeth cried, trying hard to understand what was being said.

"I believe Izzy is a psychopath, or at least a sociopath whose only true joy in life was her son. She didn't know who killed her son but thought it was one of you Vanderlin descendants. She was determined to kill her son's murderer and simply, methodically, went down the list of those that were in the house."

"Why didn't she kill us then?" Jason asked.

Frank smiled. "She liked you. Especially you, Elizabeth. She hoped that she would find out who was Benjamin's actual killer before having to kill you."

Elizabeth turned white as a sheet. "Do you mean she would have killed us as well?"

"Yes, I think so," Frank answered. "I suspect she would have killed one or both of you next. Then probably the house staff. Only then could she have been certain that she had had her justice. Thank God we found Vincent before that happened!"

"How did you find out about Vincent?" Jason asked.

"Ah, that," Frank declared. "I figured out the treasure. Once we found out that Vincent was a Vanderlin descendant like the rest of you and saw his obsession with the treasure, and of course he was the last one to see and talk to Benjamin alive, it was not a great leap to imagine him the murderer of Benjamin. The rest, as you know, was a simple trap to see if we were right."

Elizabeth and Jason looked at each other simultaneously and chorused, "You found the treasure?"

Frank smiled and nodded.

"Well?" They both blurted.

"It is not as you imagined." Frank began, "It was a matter of putting all of the clues together. First there was the inscription on the watch that belonged to James Vanderlin. Eli had written that until Vanderlin could come to admire Eli, James would never find his treasure. I think everyone believed that to be a reference to the painting of Eli in the bed-and-breakfast house on Silver Street."

Both Elizabeth and Jason nodded in understanding and agreement.

"Indeed, the clue to finding the treasure was in the painting," Frank continued. "When I went to Virginia City, I found two paintings that Vanderlin had had done of his first wife and daughter. When I saw the paintings, they looked vaguely familiar, like I had seen them before although I knew I hadn't. Then, when I went to Boston, I found a letter that Eli had written to James. The letter had been on Eli's person when he was killed but was not taken by the murderers. They were only interested in taking the watch that had belonged to James Vanderlin. The letter referred to two small pictures of James's first wife and daughter that had been in the watch and that it was the reason that Eli had stolen the watch."

Elizabeth and Jason both looked confused, and Frank could see that he was not helping clear the confusion.

"The treasure that Eli spoke of in his inscription in the watch was these two small pictures of Vanderlin's first wife and daughter. There was no gold! Vanderlin's treasure was these two small pictures, the only true images he had of his beloved wife and daughter."

"Ahhh," Elizabeth intoned, understanding finally.

"When Eli's murderers brought the watch back to Vanderlin, and Vanderlin discovered that the pictures were not there, it must have driven him mad. And Eli was dead, so Vanderlin couldn't go back and question him further. He later tried to have the pictures duplicated from memory, but they weren't very good."

"What happened to the small pictures of James's wife and daughter?" Jason asked, enthralled in the mystery.

"That's the thing!" Frank exclaimed. "They are the small pictures in Eli's portrait, the ones on either side of him in the painting! They are the actual pictures from James Vanderlin's watch—the ones he killed Eli for."

"But why didn't James come and get them?" Elizabeth asked.

"He didn't know about them," Frank answered quietly. "He never understood the inscription in the watch! He never came to Elko to look at the painting of Eli! I think James thought Eli meant personal admiration, that James would have to admit personal admiration of Eli before Eli would reveal to James the whereabouts of the pictures. But by the time James read the inscription in the watch, Eli was already dead and would never be able to reveal the whereabouts of the pictures. I'm sure James thought the pictures were lost to him forever!"

"That is so tragic!" Elizabeth sniffed, wiping her eyes. "That because these men could not communicate, everything ended so tragically!"

Frank nodded. "It so often happens that way, I'm afraid."

They all sat for a moment in silence, contemplating the mentioned events and how they affected the lives of so many. Elizabeth was the first to speak.

"What will happen to the painting now that Vincent is dead?"

Frank thought for a moment.

"I suspect it will stay with the estate of Vincent. Whoever is his next of kin will get it unless he has a will."

"If it were to come up for sale, I would like to have it!" Elizabeth declared. "It seems so a part of all that's happened. I would like to have it as a keepsake, a reminder."

"I will follow what happens and keep in touch with you," Frank answered, standing up to leave. "I would like you to have it as well."

CHAPTER 36

Virginia City (1875)

        *A*ngus McPhersen opened the door to the office in the saloon owned by James Vanderlin on E Street in Virginia City. He did this with dread. James Vanderlin had been in the office alone for the past five hours and had screamed at anyone with the temerity to knock on the door. By now, Vanderlin was likely stone-cold drunk. This had been Vanderlin's pattern for the last three years, a progressive downward spiral. Alcohol-fueled rages. Vanderlin had become isolated because of these tantrums, with few wanting to experience the man's irrational wrath. Business in the saloon had declined over the last few years, and only the opium den in the basement continued to thrive.

  This all seemed to start three years earlier when Will Tenerette and Joe Bide brought back that ill-fated watch that that punk kid had stolen. After James's wife had died and her son had stolen James's precious watch, James had sent at least twenty men out to find him and bring back the watch. Angus had been one of those men sent out. Vanderlin had neglected to mention that the reason he wanted the watch back was that it contained the only existing pictures of his first wife and daughter. The mandate to kill Eli Wilkes having been accomplished, Tenerette and Bide had brought the watch back to Vanderlin expecting to collect the five hundred dollars promised. What was unexpected was that when Vanderlin got the watch and looked inside the casing, he shot Bide dead on the spot and tried to kill Tenerette, missing only because Tenerette managed to escape through the door amidst the hail of bullets that felled his partner.

Vanderlin was considered from that time on a welcher on deals, and few men would work for him outright. Angus McPhersen was one of the few men that believed in his boss and was one of the few men privy to the explanation of why Vanderlin had entered into such a rage when he got his watch back. Most of Vanderlin's business after that point was conducted through Angus, although that happened less and less through the ensuing three years.

Vanderlin had become maudlin. He was often heard in his office crying out loud and loudly cursing life for its treatment of him. This, of course, became more prominent with the use of alcohol. Angus had often encouraged his boss to make use of the opium downstairs, hoping that the drug would induce a more manageable personality in Vanderlin, but James had not acquiesced. He liked alcohol, and he liked being angry. Angus, more often than not, became the subject of Vanderlin's venom. Vanderlin repudiated Angus for not anticipating some action or catastrophe or for not responding quickly enough to some incident that could have brought advantage or for simply being present on any arbitrary occasion.

Angus was getting tired of it. He had defended his boss even when Vanderlin was clearly in the wrong. He had listened to the complaints of other businessmen and employees and had endured the malice generated from Vanderlin's hate-filled soul. Sometimes he had to remind Vanderlin that he was owed payment and that the other employees were also owed money, always to the rebuke of Vanderlin's claim that none were worthy.

And now the last two employees of the saloon were threatening to leave unless they received their due compensation with additional moneys for having had to endure Vanderlin's ire. It had come to that. Vanderlin would have to pay them more to stay, and Angus knew that the job of selling that notion to the boss was practically impossible. Yet he had convinced them to wait for that very thing. And so he opened the door to the office and stepped inside to confront James Vanderlin.

The office was dark, being dimly lit with one kerosene lamp on the center of the desk. The curtains at both of the windows were drawn closed, and the room smelled of perspiration and alcohol. Papers were scattered about in complete disarray, and the safe was open. Vanderlin was nowhere to be seen. The place has been robbed, Angus thought immediately! Suddenly, the door behind him slammed shut, and James Vanderlin stepped out from behind it. He held a sterling silver candlestick in his hand, and his face held an evil expression.

"Boss!" Angus muttered, startled. He stepped back several paces as Vanderlin stumbled toward him, raising the candlestick. "Boss, it's me!" Angus managed to get out before the candlestick came crashing down onto his outstretched arm. Pain seared through Angus's arm and up into his shoulder. "What are you doing?" he sputtered.

James Vanderlin just kept coming, raising the candlestick and slashing at Angus with all of his might. He was properly drunk however, and his aim and stance were unsteady. Angus managed to parry the next few blows with little effort.

"Thief!" Vanderlin screamed, continuing to charge at Angus.

Angus managed to lever James's weight on the next blow and hurtled Vanderlin over the desk and against the back wall, knocking the desk lamp to the floor. Angus ran around the desk, red-faced with fury, and saw Vanderlin slumped against the wall, his head bleeding profusely from hitting the corner of the cabinet there. A small fire had started from the overturned lamp and began consuming some of the scattered papers on the floor. The fire soon gained in size as Angus stood staring at the unconscious James Vanderlin.

Angus McPhersen made no effort to put the fire out, nor did he call to anyone to do the same. Instead, he walked to the open safe, removed what cash and coin were there, and left the room muttering, "Stupid old fool!"

The saloon burned to the ground, as did the boardinghouse next door and a good portion of Virginia City. James Vanderlin was consumed in the flames that fateful day, and his house on Summit Street was quickly pillaged for whatever was worth taking. He had left no real legacy other than the future notoriety associated with his name. The remainder of his property in Virginia City and in California was simply taken over by others, with no one coming forward to contest the possessing. The sister he had left in Illinois, with whom he had no communication, never heard of his death. She had assumed he had died years earlier from his many nefarious activities, and her religious proclivities had prevented her from trying to establish contact with her wayward brother.

That James Vanderlin's name was remembered into the future and into posterity was due primarily to the one person he hated most: his stepson Eli Wilkes. It was ironic that these two, who so despised each other, would be the means to their being memorialized.